APPLE SPY
IN THE SKY

By Marc Lovell

APPLE SPY IN THE SKY
SPY ON THE RUN
THE SPY WITH HIS HEAD IN THE CLOUDS
THE SPY GAME
HAND OVER MIND
A VOICE FROM THE LIVING
THE SECOND VANETTI AFFAIR
THE BLIND HYPNOTIST
DREAMERS IN A HAUNTED HOUSE
AN ENQUIRY INTO THE EXISTENCE OF VAMPIRES
A PRESENCE IN THE HOUSE
THE IMITATION THIEVES
THE GHOST OF MEGAN

APPLE SPY IN THE SKY

MARC LOVELL

PUBLISHED FOR THE CRIME CLUB BY
DOUBLEDAY & COMPANY, INC.
GARDEN CITY, NEW YORK
1983

All of the characters in this book
are fictitious, and any resemblance
to actual persons, living or dead,
is purely coincidental.

Library of Congress Cataloging in Publication Data

Lovell, Marc.
Apple spy in the sky.

I. Title.
PR6062.O853A8   1983   823'.914
ISBN 0-385-18308-9
Library of Congress Catalog Card Number 82-45433

First Edition

Copyright © 1983 by Doubleday & Company, Inc.
All Rights Reserved
Printed in the United States of America

APPLE SPY
IN THE SKY

PROLOGUE

Dear Angus,

Here is the personal and private report you asked me for the other night at dinner, my appraisal of your man Porter in relation to what you termed a little problem in Ibiza. Not that I believe you gave me the story straight in respect of said problem. I can remember many long years ago you saying, "The quickness of the hand deceives its thumb." I doubt very much if you have changed since then. And, of course, the truth is none of my business, Official Secrets Act or not. After all, we were in different Upstairs departments for ages before I was put out to graze.

Anyway, retirement being every bit as tedious as I'd always dreaded, I was grateful for this crumb of involvement. I shall thoroughly enjoy the undercover play of sidling up to you tonight at Lucy's cocktail do and slipping this note into your pocket. You will then go to the loo, I expect, where, after reading, you will Burn and Flush.

Dear old B & F. Do you recall that night in Lisbon when we both got rather drunk and made up all manner of scandalous or obscene words to go with those initials? Ah yes. But don't get me going on reminiscence or we'll be here for hours.

Your courier came yesterday, on schedule. He politely—and quite correctly—declined to leave me alone with the photocopy of the dossier, and hid his impatience extremely well while I perused.

The dossier explains, at least, the question of why this man Appleton Porter was recruited for Intelligence in the first place. After you had given me a rough description, he sounded like someone who should have been rejected in an early sifting.

One reason is, naturally, his languages. I admit to being envious of his six perfect, five understood but spoken poorly, and seven familiar terms with. The second reason, I imagine, is that he was approached at university by dear old Professor Atwater, who is still there, I understand, recruiting for the other side. So trusty Green stepped in and enrolled Porter for the Brits. And the reason for *that* is Appleton Porter having had a romantic view of the espionage world. It was no doubt assumed that he might be inclined to throw in his lot with Atwater, simply on account of the cloak-and-dagger glamour.

Porter retains his romanticism to this day (dare I suggest that none of us is any different?), but that's no black mark, and I see that his loyalty rating is also unchanged, a solid 10. After that, the rest is all downhill.

Appleton Porter, known intimately as Apple, is six feet seven inches tall. I'm tempted to put a row of exclamation marks. How could he ever blend into the background, become one of the herd, go unnoticed in a crowd? Six-three is even too tall for an operative, in my opinion. Height alone is enough to keep your man permanently waiting in the wings. But there's more.

Porter has a sympathetic nature. He is kind to the aged and small creatures, has an atrocious habit of being able to see the other person's point of view, and falls in love at the traditional drop of a lace handkerchief. It would thus be difficult for him to be cold when the situation called for same, let alone ruthless, while at various descending levels of the scale he could be capable of letting sympathy influence his devotion to duty.

Porter has a low tolerance for alcohol. Apart from the obvious dangers, it's enough to make any member of the Service, which has its traditions to consider, reach with shocked hands for the nearest bottle. Is there something wrong with the man?

Porter, at the age of twenty-eight, has been out in the field only three times. He did not shine. Indeed, there's a little awkwardness to be read between the lines of those three reports. Nothing specific, mind you, but undeniably there. The man is not a pro.

Porter's training scores were pretty dismal. A 6 for unarmed combat, 5 for pain resistance, an indifferent 6 for lying ability, a 4 in interest in gossip. How the instructors at Damian House must have sighed. It makes me sigh myself to wonder why Porter didn't have the cunning to try and fake his ratings. Is there no guile in the man at all?

Finally, Porter blushes. He blushes often and easily. Through a talkative ex-girlfriend (I see in Attachment A, a recent addition to the dossier) it is revealed that Porter over the years has bought many so-called cures for his affliction, via advertisements in magazines. These quickly lose their power because of familiarity. The man, alas, is a terminal blusher.

I can see where Appleton Porter has been genuinely useful over the years as a linguist. He's done a lot of hard, unromantic work as a translator, has taken the interpreter's chair at many high-level and secret conferences between the Western Powers, and his job/cover at the United Kingdom Philological Institute is particularly good.

He should be allowed to continue undisturbed in the same

way, go on being a member of that league which we call the faceless ones. These people are quite unusable apart from their specialities, which might be tightrope walking or the ability to read upside down at speed. I know of one woman—she can hold her breath for almost three minutes—who has been waiting to be called into action for nigh on twenty years. That's as it should be.

If I didn't know better, Angus, I'd think that you asked for my evaluation for some other, obscure motive. You might, for instance, have been searching for a redeeming feature in the man, and have believed that I, in retirement, would be less severe than formerly. Or you could have been acting out of kindness in the giving of crumbs. You might have wanted to find out if I had gone completely senile.

And, of course, it's quite possible that I was sent the wrong dossier. I did hear on the grapevine that there had been several little errors, mere tiny disasters, in your particular department since you were elevated to Control. But these things take time, and you've been there only seven years or so.

However, enough of this friendly chat. In sum, let me say that he, Mr. Appleton Porter, is a mess. As a field operative he would make an excellent ploughman. He would certainly make a marvellous target for assassination. He is wrong for anything other than his speciality—languages. You will not, obviously, be sending this man to Ibiza.

   Yours cordially,
    Sam

CHAPTER 1

The nice thing about Ibiza town's port, Apple thought, was its un-dockland appearance. There were few of the ugly pieces of machinery that usually stood about with an attitude of threat, like people-eating robots. There was little of the grease and grime, the confusion of stacks made unhealthily mysterious by tarpaulins, the oily dross and offended-seeming response from dock workers.

Looking down from the prow of the baby ocean liner as it crept side- and nose-in to the L of wharf, Apple saw shops and sidewalk cafés fronting the old buildings. People strolled slowly in the September humidity or lounged at cafés over post-lunch coffees and brandies.

The façades of some buildings were white, others of natural stone, but white grew to total prominence as the old section of town climbed up the hillside. It looked like a mass of crouching Arabs making an attack on the summit.

Apple was glad to be arriving by sea, taking the six-hour boat trip out of Palma after flying to Mallorca, where he had cleared Spanish Customs. It made the transition more pronounced, as well as convincing him that he was actually docking at an island in the Mediterranean. He could almost believe that he was a real tourist. Certainly, he told himself, he looked like one.

That was true. With his pale, freckle-scattered complexion

and neat sandy hair, plus the expression of eagerness in his green eyes, with his new jeans and T-shirt and unscuffed sneakers, with the knapsack at his feet, Appleton Porter looked like an escapee from the world of dim offices who was about to take his two weeks of abandon in the sun.

That, the out-of-season vacation, had been simple to arrange. Apple always let his holiday time build up. He had told his superior at the United Kingdom Philological Institute:

"My Norwegian is getting rusty, Professor Warden. You know how one gets these irrational feelings of urgency. I'd like to go to Oslo at once, if that's all right with you."

The old man, who was fluent in fourteen languages, who knew nothing of Apple's Intelligence connection, had agreed and approved.

Apple had felt uncomfortable about feeding Professor Warden a lie. He would have preferred, at least, to get close to the truth, say that he wanted to study the Ibizan dialect of Catalan. But Angus Watkin would be sure to find out—as he somehow was able to unearth all things—and make sarcastic remarks about amateurism, as well as putting his underling one more step down on the Service ladder.

Apple had few dislikes, most of which embarrassed him. The only one that he considered justified was his dislike of his chief, the suave Angus Watkin. Quite right, Apple often told himself, embarrassed.

Likes, on the other hand: of these Apple had an uncountable many. Some he was able to indulge. Thought of that came to him now as, the boat throbbing to a stop, he had a closer view of the sitters and strollers below.

A good proportion were in the casual-to-outrageous style that had become synonymous with the island of Ibiza. Here was a home for lost hippies, the clothing seemed to say; it was impossible to shock or offend, to provoke odium or hilarity or scorn; so go ahead, indulge away.

Apple smiled nervously. For as long as he could remember he had needed to hold a tight rein on the rebel inside him. This anti-establishment rogue would have had him grow his hair long, wear moccasins, and, far from trying to hide the despised height, flaunt it by draping it in colourful wildness. There had even been mad moments when an earring had been hinted at.

Now's your chance, the rebel said.

Apple blinked and shook his head. He was no longer feeling a bit of a chancer for being in jeans and T-shirt instead of his usual sombre-hued suits. He felt stolid. Old. Fixed. Boring.

Bravely, however, Apple stared on at the plethora of bare feet, shredded hats, long and tangled hair, swinging jewellery, and the attempt to wear every single colour of the spectrum at the same time.

He settled on a figure that was sagged against a post. Lazily watching the boat, the man had curtain-like hair that showed little of his face except a Zapata moustache, a green/red/blue shirt the length of a topcoat, orange pants that ended raggedly at the calves, and one sandal.

Bells rang. For one startled second Apple thought they were in his head. Then he realized that they were real, and signalling disembarkation: the liner had made its last throb.

Within five minutes Apple was going down the gangway, his knapsack pulling on his shoulders, his eyes happily taking in the scene below.

Wharfside had a straggly crowd of people: meeters and hugging families; onlookers and policemen, both hoping for action; hotel couriers who ranged from the resplendently uniformed and easily identifiable to the humble displayers of name cards; more of the crazy-clad contingent.

In respect of the last, Apple helped himself with the reminder that the hippies were not, in a sense, real. They were not Ibizan but part of the large foreign colony, *extranjeros* who were determinedly doing their own wild thing for six months or a year before returning to greyness and tedium.

Apple further reminded himself of his specialness at this time. In no way was he stolid or boring. He was on a mission.

With a twinge of excitement, Apple stepped down onto the concrete. He smiled as he moved through the sparse crowd, but made his smile that of a tourist. It said:

I am visiting in all innocence, visiting to enjoy Ibiza's charm and be an ambassador of goodwill, visiting to buy souvenirs and mail off wish-you-were-here's and sample the traditional dishes. I am a lamb.

Apple winced when came the suspicion that he was able to play his role without the slightest effort. He narrowed the smile.

Among the couriers, commercial greeters, Apple spotted a woman who was holding on her chest a card that read: Royal Rose Pension. The card, buckled and scruffy, was worded in ball-point. Apple's smile became genuine, warm, as he headed for the woman.

She was about his own age. Average height, she wore faded blue jeans and a man's shirt over a plump but shapely body. Her brown hair was parted in the centre and formed into a plait at either side. She had a snub nose and blue eyes, and would have been prettier if it hadn't been for her worried expression.

She was looking around searchingly. This ended with a snap when Apple stopped in front of her. She smiled, but the worry somehow managed to linger over her features.

As if he had learned the phrase by heart, Apple chanted in bad Spanish, "I have reservation at pension."

The woman answered in English that had a faint Welsh lilt. "Then you must be Mr. Barker. How do you do. Welcome to Ibiza."

Her name was Mona Smith, Apple learned as they walked together across the quay. She had been a widow for five years, owner of the Royal Rose Pension for eight months. She had a staff of one, and this was Martha's day off.

"Hence the personal service, Mr. Barker."

"It can't be a very big place then, Mrs. Smith."

"Ten bedrooms, three baths. The minimum, in fact. The last owners, who were also British, failed in the business, and I'm just about breaking even."

"Well, that's something at least," Apple said, nodding down at the woman encouragingly.

She said, "Yes, but the tourist season's over now. It'll be a hard slog through the winter. I have only three guests at the moment. I might as well be honest and tell you I was delighted to get your telegram."

Apple hadn't been the cable's sender. He said, "Good."

"How did you come to hear about the dear old Royal Rose, by the by?"

He never had—before being told where he would be staying. Which, he thought smugly, was a perfect example of an Angus Watkin mistake. All the big sections of an operation were always worked out to the last intricate, double-dealing dot, while the side details were often left to take care of themselves. A story ought to have been provided.

"A friend," Apple lied smoothly. "He was on the island last spring and heard of the Royal Rose as a place where they served food to Anglo-Saxon tastes." It was an educated gamble.

"Yes," Mona Smith said. "I do try to keep the oiliness down."

"So I needn't worry about Spanish tummy."

"As long as you don't drink the water, no."

They had turned along the wharf's L and were now passing in front of the sidewalk cafés. Stuffing her name card in a hip pocket, Mona Smith said, "In case you haven't guessed already, my place is within walking distance of here, in the old town. Very central, as the guidebooks say."

Apple nodded. He was pleased about that fact, also that the owner was a talkative type, also that she had met him in person. The last two were particularly useful: he could learn something about the other guests even before getting to the pension.

Craftily, Apple began with the owner herself. That way he wouldn't rouse suspicion. He asked, "Have you always been in this kind of business, Mrs. Smith?"

"Sort of," she said. "And I think, as you're going to be with us for two weeks, you might as well call me Mona. We're quite informal at the Royal Rose."

She looked up at him with a grin, which, with the plaits and lack of cosmetics, made her suddenly look ten years old.

Although he didn't know why exactly, Apple almost blushed. Fighting back by laughing, he said, "Agreed. I'm Arnold, by the way. And I may stay longer than a fortnight, depending on what the weather's like."

Mona launched into a description of Ibiza's marvellous autumn climate—"So gentle, calm, kind"—and Apple mused with a sigh that, not unusually, he had managed to out-crafty himself.

Mona was extolling the mildness of early November by the time they turned away from the waterfront. They passed between a café whose outside menu board was chalked up in

German and a boutique that boasted of having the latest from New York.

"Thank you," Apple said firmly into a pause. "That's useful to know."

"Yes. So there's no need to hurry away. However, to answer your question."

Mona and her husband had operated a tea shop in a Welsh border village, she explained. After his death in a train accident she had taken a job as trainee-manager in a pub. She had been in charge of another hotel when the insurance claims were finally settled.

"I took the money and ran—to Ibiza," Mona said. "That was the end of the run. I've been ambling ever since. But I'll make it yet. All it needs is eighteen hours' labour a day."

Apple murmured sympathetically. He thought it brave of Mona Smith to look merely harried. Others would be wringing their hands. He hoped for her sake that his job would prove to be a long one.

"We turn here, Arnold."

They went onto a narrow, winding street. One-way traffic fumed along in crawls and spurts. People spilled over into the roadway from the crowded sidewalks. There were tourists in shorts, locals in sober dress, and foreign-colony members in raver drag. Every other shop sold souvenirs.

Mona said, "Your turn to tell, Arnold. How do you earn your daily bread?"

As they walked on, sometimes side by side, sometimes one behind the other, threading through the pedestrians, Apple began on his cover. He listened to himself with interest. The story was having its first outing and he was curious to hear how it sounded, also to see if he gave it with the right air of boredom.

Vaguely, Apple became aware of a noise from some way

behind. It was the peevish blast of car horns, the cry of a wounded traffic jam. Apple went on talking.

"Not the most exciting job in the world," he said. "But the fringe benefits are fairly decent."

"And you've never been married?"

Aware, again vaguely, that the horn blowing had stopped, Apple told about the three broken engagements, which he had just invented as an embroidery for the edges of his cover. It made him feel pleasantly cunning.

"What a shame," Mona said, looking up at him. They were walking side by side in the roadway. "You—" She broke off as from behind grew the roar of a car's motor. She looked back. "Hey."

Apple asked, "What?"

"Look out!" Mona shouted. At the same time, she gave him a hard push.

Apple, as good manners dictated, had been walking on the outer side. He went staggering across the road. That he kept his balance was due to bumping into a fat tourist on the opposite kerb. As he rebounded from the collision of bodies, turning, Apple saw the car flash by—and beyond it Mona standing with her hands over her eyes.

The car was a medium-sized black Seat. Its driver, hunched over the wheel, wore a multicoloured shirt. His hair, which came down to his shoulders, covered most of his face.

The next second the car had gone, sweeping around a curve in the street. Another second, and the pedestrians who had paused to watch were moving on. Apple, tense and sweaty, looked around to apologize to the fat tourist. He too was moving off.

Mona had uncovered her eyes. When a line of cars had gone by, she came hurrying across and gasped, "Are you all right?"

"Yes. Thanks to you. He must be drunk. Or blind."

"Some stupid tourist in a rented car. They think they can get away with anything."

"Looked more like a hippie resident."

"The hair, you mean?" Mona said, patting his arm as if he were a little boy in need of reassurance. "Well, you can buy wigs here on every corner. They're very popular. Some tourists like to play the Ibiza thing to the hilt. Sure you're all right?"

"Perfectly," Apple lied. His nerves were racing. "And again, many thanks."

"He was coming straight at you, seemed to me. It almost looked deliberate."

He laughed while shuffling his knapsack back into a firm position. "Who'd want to run down poor me? Probably he couldn't see properly with that curtain of hair—real or false."

"I must say you're pretty cool about it," Mona said, looking up at him admiringly. "I'd be shattered. In fact, I am. When we get to the pension I'm going to lie down and rest."

"I might just take a siesta myself," Apple said. He had told himself that Arnold Barker wasn't the type who would shrug off the incident as the kind of thing that happened every day. "Frankly, I'm not anywhere near as calm as I look."

The admiration didn't leave Mona's eyes. "That's very honest of you," she said. "I like that."

Apple tried to shrug. With the knapsack on, it was impossible. He spread his elbows.

Mona turned away. "The Royal Rose is just around the corner."

Three days before, in Kensington, Apple had left the United Kingdom Philological Institute to take his midmorning break for coffee. He headed for a nearby cafeteria. There, yesterday, Salads & Juices had given the impression of smiling at him. She was blond and attractive.

A fine drizzle was falling. As he walked, Apple repeatedly raised a flat hand to test the rain. If it grew heavier, he would put up his umbrella. But, for one thing, he liked the swashbuckle feeling of the swing and stab, for another he avoided anything that tended to increase his height.

Apple was thinking of Salads & Juices, earthily, when a taxi zoomed into the kerb at his side. The driver was looking at him expectantly. With an apologetic smile, Apple went across to explain that he hadn't been signalling for a cab, only testing the rain. He hoped the cabbie wouldn't be offended.

Before he had come to a stop, Apple recognized Ethel. She had been in government service for thirty years—after a decade of being a real taxi. She had done duty with Scotland Yard, Customs, and the Narcotic Squad, before being passed over to Intelligence.

Apple said, "I thought she'd gone to that great big scrapyard in the sky." He touched the door fondly.

"She's due for it," the driver said. He was young and forgettable, one of the herd. "She's known to every spook in the country."

"And has been for years," Apple said, showing off, playing the seasoned pro he would have liked to be. "Once a couple of Hammers with the usual diplomatic immunity, they pinched Ethel from outside one of the Upstairs buildings. When they dumped her, the back was loaded with old copies of *Pravda*."

"Cheeky bastards. Did we retaliate?"

"We sent Moscow a washer for the leaky tap they had in the basement of KGB headquarters." Although he spoke casually, he was beginning to feel excited. This approach, surely, could only mean a mission.

"Anyway, Ethel's only used nowadays when the scene is triple clean," the driver said. "Hop in."

"How do I know you're not a Hammer, or perhaps a white-slaver?"

"How do I know you're the real, genuine Appleton Porter whom old Angus is waiting impatiently to see?"

Apple got in.

The cab moved off with a series of wails and grinds. Two minutes later, after going along several streets, Ethel was brought to a stop on a corner. Apple looked out from the kerbside window. It was the other door, however, that opened, and Apple told himself that he should have known better than to expect his chief to do anything in the normal way.

"Good morning, sir."

"Morning, Porter," Angus Watkin said, lowering himself onto the seat. "We'll talk in a moment." He raised his voice for "Drive on, Fifteen."

The taxi drew away. Apple, growing more excited, craved the comfort of a cigarette. But he didn't want to rankle Watkin, who numbered smoking among his pet hates, along with Americans, Naval Intelligence, cats, and any kind of culinary endeavour that was below cordon bleu level.

Apple contented himself feebly with drumming his fingers on the handle of his umbrella. Surreptitiously, he watched Angus Watkin via his reflection in the glass behind the driver.

The man from Upstairs was average build, wearing the trilby and fawn raincoat of Mr. Everyman. His age lay somewhere between fifty and sixty. There was nothing remarkable about his face, no hint of unusual intelligence in his eyes, no suggestion of ruthlessness in the mouth. He could have passed for that man along the street whom neighbours are surprised to realize exists among them, when he has been arrested for having murdered seventeen prostitutes.

Angus Watkin asked, "Am I looking well, Porter?"

"Oh—er—yes. Yes, sir."

"You, I think, are a trifle thinner than when we last met, some months ago. Possibly you have been eating too many salads."

Christ, Apple thought, the bloody man knows everything. Or at any rate, he pretends to, which is almost as good when you're an artist at the bluff.

The driver steered Ethel through the gateway of a private house, stopped, got out, and strolled back toward the street.

Angus Watkin turned semi-sideways on the seat. As expressionless as always, he said, "Your name, until further notice, is Arnold Barker. Get that fixed. I have here a passport and other documents relating to that cover. But first, I want to tell you the picture. Ready to absorb?"

"Absolutely, sir," Apple said, feeling a tingle inside. A mission it was.

"For some time now, hard drugs in large quantities have been finding their way into British military bases both here and abroad. These narcotics are particularly cheap, but of high quality, which would seem to rule out an underworld business. What would be an alternative possibility, Mr. Barker?"

"Moscow," Apple said promptly. "The Reds trying to undermine morale and efficiency, if not create dependence. They did it in Vietnam, and they've had considerable success with the same tactics among the American forces stationed in West Germany."

"Excellent. That is precisely what we suspect. The Kremlin would have no trouble whatever in producing the drugs. The only problem would entail channelling. Do you see?"

"No, sir."

Watkin's eyes became sleepy, which meant he was enjoying himself. "Distribution would have to appear to be the work of crooks, smugglers, gangsters," he said. "The whole scheme would be spoiled if it were believed to have a political background."

"Quite, sir."

"The obvious answer, therefore, would be to channel the drugs through an established centre. One of said centres is the island of Ibiza in the Mediterranean." Angus Watkin paused. "You do know the Catalan language and its various dialects, don't you?"

"I do, sir, yes."

"Good. But forget that fact as securely as you're busy forgetting your real name—whatever that name may be."

Apple came in on cue with "It's Arnold Barker, sir."

Nodding, Watkin said, "Your knowledge of the language and of Castilian Spanish will be used for listening purposes only. You are an innocent tourist who speaks English and nothing else."

"Except, perhaps, for a few useful phrases of the type one gets from guidebooks?"

"If you wish. But do let me get on with it. I shall be late for luncheon at this rate."

"Excuse me, sir."

"One drug channel," Watkin said, "was traced back to a British-operated boarding house in Ibiza called the Royal Rose. There the trail seemed to end. We sent an operative to stay at the pension as a guest. His cover name was George Trent. That was five weeks ago. Two weeks ago, Trent stopped making contact."

Apple experienced a familiar chill in his chest. "Oh."

"He disappeared," Angus Watkin said. He might have

been talking about a pigeon. "On the surface, it appears that he left the pension with his things. The sole official note of his leaving is that the landlady complained to the British Consulate about Trent's unpaid bill."

"And he hasn't been heard of since?"

"Not a whisper. He is either dead, being held captive, or has been taken to Moscow to be pumped dry."

The first and the last were probably as good as the same, Apple mused. He asked, trying to sound unperturbed and efficient, "The local police haven't been told about this, sir?"

His chief eased away to give him a long look. It was so long that Apple eventually broke the silence with "No, of course they haven't. I don't know what I was thinking of."

Angus Watkin returned to his former position. He said, "The drug aspect you will more or less ignore. That's an expert's job, and we still don't know for sure if there is a Communist connection. Your task, as Arnold Barker, will be to try and find out what happened to George Trent."

At least, Apple thought, that might not be so dangerous as the other job. But even while thinking thus, Apple knew he wouldn't be able to resist poking into the main matter, with hopes of scoring a starry victory.

Angus Watkin reached inside his coat. "Now I'll give you your papers and tell you all about yourself."

"Yes, sir," Apple said. "And I appreciate you giving me this opportunity to show what I can do."

"I really don't have a great deal of choice in the matter," Watkin said mildly. "There's this little NATO problem on at the moment, and all my best men are occupied."

It was a standard routine, Apple mused as he lay on the bed in a post-siesta daze, naked apart from underpants. A routine that was quite usable on a normal street, but perfect when the traffic was one-way. You straddled your car on the middle line, not so much to keep the cars behind you—that was what the horn blasting had been about—as to give all vehicles ahead time enough to get well on their way. Then you had a clear field, both for the hit and the escape.

Apple opened his eyes. Lazily he roved them around his room, taking in the flowered wallpaper and Landseer prints, the corner washbasin, the bedstead of brass, the ceiling with its beams.

With dozy interest, Apple noted that a spider was coming down from the ceiling on its thread. He hoped it wouldn't tickle when it landed on his bare feet.

Closing his eyes again, Apple mused that George Trent could have been disposed of with a traffic routine—hit by a car on a country road and then buried. Someone could have sneaked into the pension and tidily removed his things.

After checking with one eye that the spider wasn't in danger of falling and hurting itself, Apple told himself that the driver of the black car could, of course, have been drunk. He could also have been the same hippie who had observed the boat's docking. And if he was, that didn't mean a definite connection with anything: Trent, drugs, himself.

Trouble was, Apple thought, a good proportion of the men around here wore Zapata moustaches, a lot had shoulder-length hair, and many had both. Also, both could be bought on any corner.

Opening his eyes again, Apple wondered if he should try to trace the black car.

It was then that he noticed the knot. The sleep haze going from his vision, he could see better. What he saw was that the spider's thread had a knot in it.

Spiders were clever, Apple knew, but there were limits. He looked up from the centrally placed knot with its two ears of ends; up to where the thread met the ceiling. There was no web. Instead, a coin-sized hole showed between the beams.

Apple brought his vision back down, right to the other extreme. The insect, descending slowly, was two or three inches above his left leg.

He tensed. His eyes fully free of sleep now, he could see with full clarity. That was no spider. It was a scorpion.

One second after Apple had made his identification, he saw and felt the landing. The insect was on his naked ankle.

Keeping rigidly still, Apple reminded himself that the Mediterranean scorpion, an inch and a half long at the most, was not capable of killing. The poison of its sting was merely debilitating.

Merely, Apple thought. He could be rendered unconscious. He would be at anyone's mercy. He could be killed or taken away by night and shipped to a place of interrogation. Was this the answer to the disappearance of George Trent?

Apple, his heart tapping rapidly, squinted down without moving his head; without moving any muscle save those of his eyes. He watched the scorpion as it crept slowly up his shin. It tickled.

If I laugh, he self-warned, I've had it. Noise or movement would be taken as a sign of attack. The pincers on that upcurled tail would jab down into the flesh and venom would flow through from the sac in the abdomen.

Apple sighed. Sometimes he wished he didn't have a love for collecting odd bits and pieces of information. There were some facts he could nicely do without knowing. In this case, the uninformed would simply kick the creature off, and probably get away with it. A little learning was a dangerous thing.

The thread, Apple thought, his worry pausing. It was still attached. If he could pull it aside, the scorpion would be taken along as well.

Holding his breath, Apple carefully began to raise his right leg. When it was clear of the bedding, he swung it away as he went on lifting. He began to bend his knee. This he ended on noting with alarm that the scorpion had stopped moving.

Apple let his breath go out in a long, slow, soothing hiss. The insect remained perfectly still. Its tail was curved as threateningly as an angry cat's back.

Apple decided not to wait any longer. The raised leg would have to be bent enough, suffice as a trajectory.

Aiming, he kicked.

His foot hit the thread and carried it on. The scorpion was jerked upward. Apple flung himself into a sideways roll. He shot off the bed's edge and crashed to the floor.

At the moment when the noise of his action finished, he heard a scuffle of movement from above, beyond the ceiling beams. He jumped to his feet.

Noting that the scorpion was on his bed, Apple leapt for the door. He had it open and was midway through before remembering that he wore nothing but a pair of underpants. Modesty sent him stumbling toward the chair that held his clothes.

Hopping, furious with himself, Apple struggled into jeans. He fastened and zipped them as he went back to the door, out and along the passage. At its end were the tile-clad stairs. Bare feet slapping, he charged upward, and on the level went along to the room that would be directly above his own.

The door was open. Apple went in. The room's bare neatness showed that it was presently without a guest. Getting down on his hands and knees, Apple looked under the bed. He found the hole. He peered through it one-eyed and saw his bed below, with the scorpion still there.

Hurrying, he left the room and went to others. Their doors

were locked, except that to the bathroom, which was deserted. He went back to the stairs and up a final, narrow flight.

At the top were two doors. One was locked, the other stood ajar and led into a small, stuffy storeroom. Apple looked around with interest, settling now from his haste: he knew he had failed to corner whoever it was that had lowered the scorpion.

But there was nothing among the dusty boxes and mildewed suitcases to make Apple's interest quicken. Doubly disappointed, he plodded back downstairs to his own floor.

On it he nearly bumped into a girl. She was swinging onto the bottom step as he was swinging off it. They both eased back and said, "Sorry."

The girl, about twenty years old, was big and hefty, packing to the stitch-strain limit her trouser suit. She had short curly hair, small eyes, a face as broad as it was long, and the slab chin of a boxer. Even the dangling earrings and the collar of necklaces couldn't make pretty what was so absolute in its big plainness.

"Hello," Apple said. "I've just moved in. Arnold Barker."

"Martha March. Hello. I work here." Her manner was pleasant, her accent New Zealand. "Have you lost your way in this great mansion of a place?"

Apple smiled. "No, but perhaps you could tell me something."

"Not likely," Martha March said, her face becoming blank, her large body straightening. "This is my day off."

"I quite understand, Miss March, that—"

"Martha," the girl said. "I'm not an old maid, y'know."

Apple shoook his head. "Of course not. No. Not at all."

"Thank you."

"I just wanted to know, Martha, what one does with scorpions. There's one in my room."

"Ask me tomorrow," Martha said, going past him and onto the stairs. "Bye."

Cool from a shower, Apple went down to the businesslike lobby. It had a floor of black and white tiles in checkerboard formation, grimly upright chairs, a small reception desk on which stood a vase of red roses.

There were glass double doors on each side; one led to a dining room, one to the street entrance, one to a bar, and one to the interior patio. That was where Apple headed, looking for signs of life.

He had dealt with the scorpion finally. Holding it up by the thread, he had spent some time in admiring the nerve of whoever had tied it at what would have needed to be close range. Next he had searched his soul and concluded that he couldn't be callous enough to endanger the insect's life by flushing it down the toilet. Last, after carefully weighing all possibilities, he had taken his captive up to the storeroom, where he had set it free by burning through the thread's end with the cinder of his cigarette. Sweating with the trauma of it all, he had headed for the bathroom shower.

The patio furniture was more inviting than that of the lobby. Tables and chairs of cane were spread around among the corner palm trees, potted plants, and the bursts of bougainvillaea that hung from walls. On a T-perch sat a green parrot.

Despite looking to be hunched in sleep, the parrot spoke. It said, "Dope."

Another voice said, "Don't mind Perky. He calls everyone a dope or a fink."

Apple turned to see a man entering from the lobby. His appearance matched the American voice. Middle-aged and lean, grey hair cut rug-short, he wore chinos and a cowboy shirt in fawn gabardine. His hawk face was deeply tanned except around the crafty blue eyes.

While putting on sunglasses he added, "Perky's been here longer than Mrs. Arkwright. He thinks he owns the joint."

"Dope," the parrot creaked.

Apple introduced himself and shook hands with the man, who said, "Harold P. Lewis. Call me Harry, huh, Arnold? I been at the Royal Rose for three months, taking life easy. Maybe I'll hang around another month or so."

Smiling, Apple said, "You must be loaded, Harry."

The man put on one of those earnest expressions that Apple always associated with Americans; he sometimes wondered if U.S. schools gave a course in Emotion Projection.

"Arnold, I'll tell you, I'm okay for bread. Not rich, not poor. I guess you could say I was comfortable."

"That must be nice."

"See, I own three hardware stores in Philly, and the managers I got in there only rob me half blind."

The parrot hissed, "Bloody dope."

Harry Lewis: "Usually he only swears for Mrs. Arkwright."

"Who's she?"

"Arnold, she's been staying in this joint for ever. Awful old bag. Keep out of her clutches or she'll bore you into your grave. More than one guest's been driven away from the Royal Rose by the gab of old Arkwright. I don't know why poor Mona doesn't give her the shove."

"I imagine she can't afford to," Apple said. He switched topics with "You must know the local ropes by this time. Maybe you could tell me where's the best place to rent a car."

The American shrugged. "All about the same. But listen, I'll give you the addresses." With glib movements he unclipped a pen from his shirt pocket and from one on his hip brought out a pad.

In a minute Apple had a list of six names, two of which were the ubiquitous Hertz and Avis. The others sounded local. As Harry Lewis had seemed to respond normally, Apple didn't press the matter of cars. He was about to mention insects when the other man asked, "How about a drink before dinner?"

"Harry, you just show me the way."

The bar was small and cosy. It pretended to be an English pub, with above the crescent of counter a shelf from which hung pewter mugs, with a scattering of brassware, and with Union Jack curtains at the windows.

Harry went behind the counter. "Mona let the bar boy go, now that the season's over. It's self-service from here on."

"She did say the Royal Rose was informal."

"Right. So what'll you have, Arnold?"

Apple named his favourite drink, sherry on the rocks. Making a poor job of hiding a grimace, Harry filled the order and then poured himself a scotch. With money put in the till, he offered cigarettes from a box.

Apple, supplying the light, asked, "Were most of the guests British here during the season?"

"Arnold, they were. All, I'd say. I was sure the only Yank. But that was fine with me. I get along with Limeys. I lived among 'em for years during the war."

Sergeant H. P. Lewis' life on a Norfolk airfield lasted through two more cigarettes and into a second drink. Apple didn't mind that, nor the fact that he had been sidetracked from leading the talk toward George Trent. He was content with his curiosity about the man he could see through the window.

Lounging in a doorway across the street, the man was apparently offering for sale the wooden dolls that stood by his sandalled feet. He had long hair and a Zapata moustache, a red and blue patchwork shirt, scruffy denim shorts that came to his knees.

Not being able to turn back the pages of his mind in this particular respect, Apple didn't know if the man was the one who had been watching the boat's arrival, and who may have been the driver of the black car. But he liked the idea.

When Sergeant Lewis was getting close to D-Day, Apple asked, "The vendor over there, is that his regular pitch?"

Harry glanced out. "Arnold, I couldn't say. There's hundreds of 'em in Ibiza town. Mostly Argentinians—don't ask me why. They sell all over the place, and a big bunch have an evening street market a couple of blocks from here."

"He doesn't seem to be doing much business."

"No, but let me tell you about that jeep of mine."

Harry had started on his third drink, Apple was still nursing the remains of his second, and the hippie hadn't changed his position or found a buyer, when there came a noise like a can being kicked along the road.

The American said, "That's the dinner gong. It's cracked."

"It sounds totally mad."

"Mona only uses it when she's serving in the patio. Which she does to impress newcomers. Yourself in this case. Tomorrow we'll be back inside, where it's nearer the kitchen."

"Anywhere's fine with me," Apple said. He drained his glass and put it down. "Harry, I'll see you later."

Right from the beginning, dinner promised to be an odd experience. The four guests sat at separate tables, one on each side of the patio. With interjections from the parrot, three of the people proceeded to have an erratic, loud-voiced conversation. The fourth guest remained silent apart from grunted answers to direct questions.

Addressed as Jason by Harry Lewis and Mona, as Mr. Lock by Mrs. Arkwright, the man was seeable only as a pair of hands. They were holding up the newspaper which he kept in front of him at all times. Even when turning pages of his *Guardian*, Jason Lock managed to stay hidden.

Mona, looking extra harried, bustled in and out with plates. Her plaits bounced, swung, trembled. Apple had a hard time stopping himself from offering to help, which was something that tourist Arnold Barker would never have spoiled his vacation by doing. He eased his urge by glaring at Martha March whenever she appeared briefly in the doorway to smile at the scurried serving.

Over the steamed fish, Mrs. Arkwright called out, "And what do you *do*, Mr. Barker? I'm sure it must be connected with your unnatural height, if I may be perfectly frank."

"There's no connection, no."

"Pity, that," the Englishwoman said. "One should always try to utilize what God has seen fit to bestow."

Apple called, "I'm sure you're right, ma'am."

"Otherwise, one might fail."

"One might."

Mrs. Arkwright took another huge mouthful of fish. She was short and stout and neckless. Her age could have been eighty. Wisps of white hair peeked from under a cloche hat, the same mauve as the loose-fitting dress that reached her booted ankles. She wore a thick mask of cosmetics, blacks and bright reds against a pure white base. Her eyes looked yellow and sinister.

Harry Lewis shouted, "Say, Alicia, did I ever tell you about that job I had in Trenton?"

Ignoring him, Mrs. Arkwright said, "I, Mr. Barker, have

been at the Royal Rose for twenty years. I have seen no less than fourteen owners come and go. They always fail." She smiled at Mona, who was passing: "Lovely fish, dear."

"Thanks, Alicia."

The parrot said, "Bleeding dope."

The man behind the newspaper grunted, Harry went on to tell of the job, Mrs. Arkwright talked about failure, Martha appeared, smiled, left.

Coming to take Apple's plate, Mona said quietly, "I'll bring my sandwich and have it here with you, if that's all right."

"I'd be honoured. Is a sandwich all you're having?"

"No time for anything else. Anyway, you know what they say: the chef at Maxim's goes home to cheese on toast." She bustled on.

Presently Mrs. Arkwright, getting a cross-signal from the American, called to Apple, "Retailing, did you say you worked in?"

"No, ma'am. Husbandry." He went on to tell of his overseer work at a government-sponsored experimental farm—which existed, and which would back up his story if anyone checked. He was aware that all three of the other guests were listening with care. The *Guardian* was perfectly still.

"I have an old cottage nearby, in Nether Weald. It's quaint without being cute." Anyone asking at the cottage, which was owned by Upstairs, would learn that its tenant was one Arnold Barker, at present abroad.

"Farming's interesting," Harry said, resettling his sunglasses. "What's that new antidote I read of the other day for hoof-and-mouth disease? Any good?"

Smiling, Apple held up a staying hand. "Please. No shop. I'm on holiday."

"Quite so," Mrs. Arkwright said. "And for your information, Mr. Lewis, it's *foot*, not *hoof*."

They went on to have a shouted discussion about British and U.S. terminology. Apple, eating his steak pie, had the feeling that he was watching a stage play. There was an element of farce in everything about the scene, even to Jason Lock sitting there like a prompter. Was the whole thing a performance, everyone here an actor/conspirator?

Thoughtful, Apple declined to be drawn into any of the talk that followed. When, soon, he turned back from watching Mrs. Arkwright stump out with the help of a cane, he saw that the invisible Jason Lock had gone from his table.

Next it was the American's turn to leave. He did so after coming over to give Apple another long warning about getting involved with a bore like Alicia Arkwright.

As Harry went out, Mona came in. She had a sandwich for herself, an apple for Apple. He said, as he had often said before throughout his life, speaking from habit, "Nature to match name."

Mona smiled at him quizzically as she sat. "What does that mean, Arnold?"

Confused, appalled at his slip, Apple fumbled into an invention about a particular type of apple called the Golden Barker. For punctuation he took large, loud bites of the fruit.

Mona nodded indifferently, concentrating on her sandwich, after saying, "It's from Alicia's private stock. She told me I could give you one."

At last Apple escaped into a question. "What's she like— Mrs. Arkwright?"

"Bit of a tyrant. A gossip. Sort of ruthless in a way. But she does have some good points. One being that she's got pots of money. Aren't I awful?"

"Not at all," Apple said. He asked about Harry Lewis—hearing what he'd already garnered from the man himself—before getting to the mysterious Mr. Lock.

Mona said, "Jason's a sweetie. As kind as could be and quite shy. Been here six months. He was a dentist in London but retired fairly early because the work was getting on his nerves."

Apple held back from saying that, among professional people, dentists had the highest rate of suicide. He didn't know why he had retained this fact in the first place.

Mona continued to talk affectionately of Jason Lock. She finished her sandwich, sat on for a moment, and then got up with a remark about idle hands. From a shelf she fetched a knitting bag. Apple told her she worked too hard.

"Good for the soul," Mona said, setting to with the needles. "Also, I sell these scarves to a souvenir shop."

The talk turned to tourism. Apple began to get restless. The night was a young shadow and he was eager to be out and about on the hunt, though he had no idea what his next step would be.

After a while he said, "Well, I think I'll stroll out, see what the night life here has to offer."

"I know of a nice little café where—"

The explosion was loud. It made Apple, who had been midway to his feet, shoot the rest of the way as he went into a jump. He jumped in the opposite direction from the noise, which had been behind him.

When Apple stopped and turned, Mona was at his side, a hand on his arm. They both stared at the shattered plant pot. With earth starred out on all sides, and a geranium in the middle, it lay behind the chair on which Apple had been sitting.

He looked up when Mona pointed. "It fell from there,"

she said. "A bathroom." The window ledge was twenty feet high. "My God, Arnold, you could've had your brains knocked out."

Apple nodded. He felt slightly sick. Mona, he noted, looked the way he felt. She said, "My fault. This kind of thing's happened before."

"How?"

"I go on pouring water in the pots and forget that the weight slowly inches them outward."

Harry Lewis came hurrying into the patio, his sunglasses held up from his eyes. "What the hell was that?"

Mona had hardly begun on an explanation when Martha March arrived, followed by a remarkably quick-moving Mrs. Arkwright. In the confusion, Apple sidled away.

An hour later, shock and nausea long gone, Apple was on a narrow, night-dark street, walking in the old part of town. He had made a brief call at the car-rental agencies, where every clerk had the same reply to his question: no, they had cars of almost every colour except black, a shade that tourists tended to avoid.

There were, however, smaller agencies to be found in the suburbs, one-man affairs which Apple thought would be more attractive to someone with any kind of villainy in mind.

But he reminded himself now that the car incident was no more certain an attempt on his life or limb than had been the falling plant pot; only his melodramatic turn of mind wanted them to be.

Apple countered with the fact that those two could-be innocuous events had been separated by one which couldn't possibly have been anything other than deliberate, the dangled scorpion, strengthening the theory that they were not only of the same ilk but of the same authorship.

And why? Were they real attempts to get him permanently out of the way, or planned near-misses that would warn or frighten him off?

Also, were there going to be more? Was it safe to stay on at the Royal Rose, safe even to remain in Ibiza?

Apple sighed cheerfully. He had no answers. All he knew, or at least sensed, was that he was in the thick of an operation, and nothing could have suited him better.

Turning a corner, Apple found he had come to the evening market. On a traffic-free street, the stalls were set up along either side in front of the closed stores. Naked bulbs glared down on the goods, all of which came under the blanket term of Arts & Crafts. It was a large blanket.

The range went from the genuine to the phony, Apple saw as he browsed at a stroll; from artisan pieces in leather, wood, or clay, to junk jewellery, plastic flowers, and mass-produced objects with an additional coating of paint. Their vendors matched in type. While all were far from conventional, some looked as if they had scuffled into the first to-hand garment without giving it a thought, others had patently dressed with great attention given to creating the right effect.

Apple had seen no wooden dolls by the time he stopped near the line's end, held there by a vendor's importuning. The woman was stout and middle-aged, wearing shredded denims and a top hat. Her small display of goods consisted of brooches of gold wire formed into names. A notice in five languages said that any name could be made while you waited.

The woman spoke a little English—learned, she said, at school in Buenos Aires. Apple agreed to purchase, and after a moment's blankness of mind came up with "Mona." While the name was being skillfully wrought with pliers, he asked about dolls. The woman knew of no one who made or sold them.

Strolling on with the brooch pocketed, Apple was reminded of the slip he had made earlier over his name and the apple. He realized with surprise that he hadn't blushed.

That, Apple thought, could be because he had been too aghast at himself, or because he was finally improving (slim hope), or because the latest treatment was having a long-term effect rather than only at the moment of blushing, though the advertiser had claimed no more than that.

This method was to imagine that you were Tom Brown, in the famous scene from his *School Days* when the odious Flashman and others pressed the seat of his pants toward an open fire. The heat would rush from face to buttocks, where a blush was quite acceptable.

It was his top, not his bottom, that next occupied Apple's mind. Between the shoulder blades had come a familiar sensation. It was a coolness. It meant that he was being watched and perhaps followed.

To establish either the casual or the determined, Apple turned off into a passageway. A yard across, it climbed and then became steps, flattened to level again on reaching another street. The cool, tickling sensation had gone.

It returned a moment later.

Not looking behind as he ambled on through the scattering of pedestrians, Apple thought unavoidably of the hippie vendor. He had been absent from his post when Apple had peered out before emerging from the pension. But, there being several darkly deep doorways, Apple had waited until a truck had rumbled by and used it as cover to get away.

Apple strolled for another five minutes, the cool sensation persisting. Finally he decided on action. He slipped into an alley, broke into a run, quickly made a circuit that brought him back onto the same poorly lit street.

Pace casual again, he went on toward where he had cut

off. He could see no one familiar ahead. There was nobody at all in wild dress. Apple wondered if once again he had been fooled by his eagerness to believe the worst. He noted that the sensation was dead.

Near the alley's mouth stood only a prosaic figure, a thin man in tropical whites and a Panama hat. He had been facing the other way, but turned now as Apple drew abreast. Body twitching, he said, "Oh, there you are. No, I mean fancy meeting you here. We should, after all, have met elsewhere."

Apple asked, "Are you talking to me, sir?"

"Of course, Mr. Barker. Good evening."

The sidewalk café was on a wharf. The tables were crowded, the private yachts across the cobbles lent a note of luxury, the passers-by were full of dinner-wine gaiety.

"A romantic scene, Mr. Barker."

"It is, Mr. Lock. I'm not surprised that you've decided to spend your retirement years here."

"I haven't, not fully. I shall have to see if the winter is as damp and chilling as the locals claim."

"You speak Spanish?"

"I'm taking lessons," Jason Lock said. He was in his early fifties, a thin-faced man with a prim mouth and timid eyes. His Hitler moustache was the same silver as his neat, flat hair. The whiteness of his clothing continued even to shoes and socks, shirt and tie. "One hour every afternoon at a language school."

The waiter came to leave their orders, milk for Jason Lock, coffee for Apple, who knew that the caffeine wouldn't keep him awake tonight. It had been a long, exciting, and nerve-squeezing day. He disguised a yawn by smiling twistedly.

"Yes, I agree, it's a pleasant outlook," Jason Lock said. He gave a smile that was tentative, as if he thought someone might grab it and run. "Jolly."

Apple nodded. "Yes. But one could hardly make a career of this. And one hour a day studying a language is only a drop in the bucket. So, Mr. Lock, how do you pass your days away?"

The Englishman's eyes took on a smug look. "I watch the world around me," he said. "In fine, I study people."

"Is that right?"

"I am, if I may state it, rather perceptive."

"You may indeed," Apple said. He had decided not to ask Lock why he had been following, was pretending to accept that their meeting had been accidental. He thought he might learn more by playing the innocent.

"I can see, Mr. Lock, that you're a man who wouldn't judge merely by appearances." Don't overdo it, he warned himself.

"That's it, in a nutshell. I try to probe beyond the façade. For instance, I have the feeling that there's more to your presence at the Royal Rose than meets the eye."

Apple took a sip of his coffee. Putting the cup down with care, he said, "I suppose someone was bound to see through the performance."

Jason Lock leaned forward with a faint intake of breath. "I was right then, mm?"

Voice and manner dull, gaze down, Apple told of his fiancée, Jane, who had jilted him to go to live with his best friend, and of the doctor who had worked the stomach pump, and of the psychiatrist who had advised a holiday abroad as the best cure for a broken heart.

Lock had leaned back, was finding his milk more interesting than the story, by the time Apple finished with "And it seems to be working." He roused himself brightly. "I haven't thought of Jane once today. Isn't that marvellous?"

"I really wouldn't know, Mr. Barker. Myself, I have managed to avoid passion all my life. Being perceptive has been a great help in that direction."

After waiting for a group of noisy revellers to weave past, Apple asked, "What do you perceive about Mrs. Arkwright?"

"The in-depth study I have made of Alicia, Mr. Barker, shows a personality quite different from that which she presents to the world." He talked on at length about the Englishwoman's true nature, which he presented as being of the shrinking-violet type.

He needed no prompting to next take up the subject of another of the pension's characters. Apple learned that Mona Smith was as hard as nails, never worried about a thing, and was indifferent as to whether or not the Royal Rose was a success, which it could be if the owner would only use a little more elbow grease.

Jason Lock hesitated. "Yes?" Apple asked casually, getting out a crumpled packet of cigarettes from his jeans. He offered it, got a declination, lit up. His next offering, a lie, was accepted with an eagerness which, for the dry ex-dentist, was probably florid.

Apple said, "I'm not so sure about Mr. Lewis."

"Ah yes. Our pseudo-American."

"Pseudo, Mr. Lock?"

"That is the prefix I used, Mr. Barker. I cannot, however, prove its truth. Indeed, I may be wrong. But I so rarely am that it's hardly worth considering."

"So you think he's a phony?"

"I do. More by perception than hard proof, admittedly. But

there was one little pointer some time ago. It convinced me that our Harry is, in fact, a Cockney."

"That's quite a long stride in accents, Mr. Lock," Apple said. He smothered another yawn.

"Perhaps. Still, what happened was, in talking about cooking, he dropped an aitch. He said *'erb* instead of *herb*."

Apple didn't bother to mention that the former was the word's correct U.S. pronunciation. He was beginning to see Jason Lock as a harmless crank and neurotic, a bachelor with the common old-maid syndrome.

Lock was leaning forward again. He seemed to have been made more eager by his listener's lack of interest. Smoothing down his white tie, as if urging control on himself, he said, "This evening—you heard him yourself—Harry Lewis made a pointless reference to a town in the United States. He did it more than once. The town was Trenton. Remember?"

"Vaguely," Apple said, and now he needed to act the casualness. "But I don't understand what you're getting at."

The ex-dentist moved his glass out of the way. "Several weeks ago we had a guest at the Royal Rose. British, it seemed. Bookseller, he said. Tourist, he claimed. That man and Harry Lewis were friendly."

"I'm still not with you, Mr. Lock."

"About three weeks ago, that man did a moonlight flit. One minute he was there, the next minute gone. And his name, Mr. Barker, was Trent. George Trent. Now do you see?"

Apple blew out a long stream of smoke. He said, "I see the similarity between Trent and Trenton, if that's what you mean. But nothing else."

"For me, that is enough. Most significant. As Harry Lewis had never mentioned the town before, why now, if not for the benefit of the latest guest?"

"For my benefit, Mr. Lock? Hardly. I've never heard of either the town or the moonlight flitter."

The man in white nodded a mild craftiness. "I think he was testing you. You know the kind of thing. Like spies exchanging secret passwords to identify themselves."

"Is that right?" Apple said. "Have you ever been involved in espionage?"

Jason Lock said, "Oh no." He leaned away. "Not at all."

"Pity. It must be very exciting. But don't let me interrupt you. Just what do you think Harry thinks I am, or what do you think *he* is?"

Lock moved his glass of milk back into place in front of him. "As to that, Mr. Barker, I'm not sure. In fact, I have no idea. As I pointed out, I'm merely an observer."

One, Apple mused, who would bear a little observing himself, though he was probably all that he seemed. Time would tell.

Apple let the approaching yawn flourish. He stubbed out his cigarette and got up. "A most interesting chat, Mr. Lock. We will talk again, I hope. I'd like to hear more about this mysterious George Trenton." He felt pleased with himself for the deliberate, allaying mistake. "But now I'm ready for sleep. Good night to you, Mr. Lock."

The ex-dentist looked flaccidly disappointed. "Good night to you, Mr. Barker."

Apple came turgidly to the surface of consciousness. He was aware in a dull sort of way that what had brought him out of his dream of Amazons was a noise. Rather, a collection of noises. It was silent now. He blinked slowly; and from the darkness his eyes met, he judged it to be the middle of the night.

Apple almost shot to full alertness on thinking of a connection between the sounds and the scorpion. But he recalled that, before retiring, he had moved his bed from under the hole in the ceiling.

Whimpering in comfort, he shuffled into a new position. He dozily listened as the noises started again. They were not furtive. There were footsteps, a door opening, a woman's laugh.

Apple became intrigued. He rolled onto his back the better to hear. By the time the noises had faded off into the waiting silence, he was fully awake. Annoyed, he sat up.

The silence continuing, firm, Apple put on the bedside lamp. He got up and lit a cigarette. Smoking, he paced. When he was down to the stub, he squashed it out with a nod. He put on his jeans. He was no longer annoyed.

The door opened quietly to his touch. Barefoot, he went out into the passage. A glow from somewhere below supplied enough light for him to see his way. He padded along to the stairs and went down.

The light came from a small lamp on the reception desk. Apple went there, into the scent from the vase of red roses. He opened the register as he swung it around. The last entry, with today's date, had been made by a Maria Sola of Barcelona.

Apple began flipping backwards through the book. Not finding what he was looking for, he returned to today and started again, going slowly. This time, although he still didn't find the expected, he did discover the reason for the lack: a jagged edge close to the ledger's spine. The page bearing the entry by George Trent had been ripped out.

CHAPTER 2

"It's Lipton's," Martha said. "I hope that's all right."

"Fine," Apple said, even though he vastly preferred Typhoo to any other kind of tea. He had tried all of them over the years and as far as his own taste was concerned none equalled Typhoo for bouquet, tone, vigour, and that inner core of friendliness. At home, he had put down in his larder a stock of the good months, April and May, with one or two Junes for their noted impertinence.

Large, plain Martha folded her arms. "And how do you like it, sir?" She was standing beside his table in the dining room, which they had to themselves. Already she had said, "They're a bunch of lie-abeds around here."

Apple put his elbows on the table and made a steeple of his fingers. With eyes slightly narrowed he said, "When the kettle's singing—almost boiling—pour an inch of water into the pot as a warmer. After emptying it out, put in the tea leaves—loose, of course, never bags."

Martha shook her head. "Of course not." Although she still wore her trouser suit, the jewellery had gone.

"Put in one spoon for me, half a spoon for the pot. By now, the kettle will be boiling. Take the pot to it, not the kettle to the pot, and add precisely one half pint of the still-bubbling water. Then let it draw for thirty seconds before bringing it here to me."

"Milk or lemon, sir?"

"Milk, please." He smiled whimsically at the absurd notion of lemon in tea. Martha March returned the smile. They understood one another.

"A cosy, sir?"

"I—um—think not," Apple said judiciously. "Not this morning." A cover over the pot would increase the strength of the contents, making for an unnecessarily stimulating beverage.

"Very good, sir," Martha said. "Well, now that brekker's settled, what was it you wanted to ask me yesterday afternoon?"

Apple unsteepled his hands. "I don't remember."

"Something about a scorpion, I think."

"Oh yes." He went on to tell of finding one in his room, under a chair, and wondering how to get rid of it. "Finally I threw it out of the window."

"Poor little thing. It was probably asleep. They're nocturnal, you know. Next time just leave it to its snooze. Okay? Now if you'll excuse me, sir."

"Arnold's the name," Apple said. "I'm not an old bachelor."

"Righto, Arnie. Stand by for the grub."

After Martha had heavily left the room, Apple got up and sidled over toward the window. He stopped when near enough to get a clear view of the area across the street. He was pleased to see that his hippie had taken up his post, leaning as before and with the dolls at his feet. Apple scrutinized the man, but there was too much hair to give a good idea of what the face looked like.

"Good morning, Arnold."

Apple made a casual turn. "Good morning," he said, heading back for his table.

Mona met him there. She was smiling shyly. Patting the upper chest of her shirt, she said, "Thank you. I just found it on the desk. How sweet and thoughtful of you."

Apple nodded at the name brooch. "I'm glad you like it."

"Oh, I do," led to more enthusiasm for the gift, following which Mona said, "Now no one can make a mistake and call me Bill."

"Nobody, Mona, could *ever* mistake you for a man."

She blinked and weaved. "Heavens. Compliments as well as presents. I swear you'll turn my head." She gestured confusedly with both hands. "But do sit down, Arnold. And do, by all means, complain like hell if you were disturbed during the wee hours."

"Why, no," Apple said, sitting. "I slept like a log."

"Oh, good. Only I had a new guest roll up. It seemed to me we were making an awful lot of noise."

"An English tourist, I suppose."

"Spanish, actually," Mona said, her expression assuming its cast of worry. "An entertainer."

Martha came in with a tray. Onto the table she began to unload every traditional item of the Bountiful British Breakfast, which Apple eyed greedily. His sole reservation, a minor one, was that the marmalade was the standard, orange, rather than his favourite, lemon.

After telling him to eat hearty, Mona went out with Martha, who was making the right sounds about the brooch.

Apple set to. Apart from the fruit juice, which smelled odd and which he emptied into a nearby plant pot, the meal was as good as it looked. He ate with only passing thoughts elsewhere: Martha March's knowledge of insects, the new guest, the apparently pointless and stupid removal of a page from the register, the fact that Hippie could be not one man but several.

Toast and corn flakes gone, the egg, ham, sausage, kidney, and tomato reduced to a vague colour scheme, Apple poured himself a second cup of tea. It was an excellent brew. In fact, he thought it was as good as any he had ever tasted. Almost, he amended, feeling a tinge of disloyalty for liking Lipton's at the expense of Typhoo. He added more milk.

Lighting a cigarette, that first and best of the day, Apple slouched back in his seat feeling the complete voluptuary. This, he thought, was the life.

Martha returned. She asked about every item of the breakfast, repeating, "Sure it was all right?" He answered that it was and told her she was a three-star cook, one who, obviously, had had plenty of practice.

From there it was an easy step to the story of an Auckland girl who, two years ago, tired of typing names for the telephone company, had set off to work her way around the world, learning as she went everything about being a household slave.

"It's the only easy way you can get a job without a work permit," Martha said. She grinned proudly. "I've been illegally employed in eight different countries."

"Good for you," Apple said, not with comfort. "But is the pay worthwhile?"

"It's putrid, Arnie. Mona's got me at half the going rate. Poor soul couldn't afford help otherwise. It'll suit me for another month or so, then I'm off to Italy."

"How do you manage for languages?"

"Esperanto."

In the doorway appeared Harry Lewis. He stayed there to lift his sunglasses and look at Apple solemnly. Dropping the glasses back over his pale-circled eyes, he moved on.

"Going for his *Herald Tribune*," Martha said. "Can't eat

brekker without it." She stepped away. "Now I'd better give that rubber plant some water before it turns into a flat tyre."

Apple stubbed his cigarette. As he began to get up, a burst of singing came from somewhere beyond the lobby.

First a leg appeared. It was long and shapely, beginning in a high-heel shoe and ending at the hem of a short, short skirt. Next came the other leg. It appeared sinuously, matched to the languid rhythm of the singing.

Apple, standing in the lobby, gazed up at the staircase with his mouth partly open. He was unaware of raising both hands to check the neatness of hair and collar.

Swaying hips, a small waist, a more than generous bosom, a mass of thick dark hair—and the whole woman had come into view at the top of the stairs. Still singing, eyes directed upward, she continued her oscillating descent.

She was in her early twenties. Her complexion had the soothing colour of a fading tan, her teeth were white enough to give off glints of light, her mouth was advertising its sensuous fullness with a crimson cosmetic. Aided by dark eyes and a petite nose, the woman was brazenly attractive.

Apple swallowed noisily. It happened in the silence after a sung phrase. The next phrase the woman broke off as she stopped and looked down. She was near the foot of the stairs. Her eyebrows rose questioningly.

After a moment's hesitation, Apple started to applaud. He slapped his hands together vigorously while wearing a fierce smile to hide the fact that he was feeling foolish, or to give the impression that he did this kind of crazy thing all the time; he wasn't sure which.

Other clapping sounded. It was slow, turgid, dragging back on the beat Apple was making. He glanced behind. Near the desk, Mona was limp-applauding. Boredom seemed to have been added to her normal expression.

Eyebrows still raised grandly, the singer made a royal gesture to bring the applause to a close. She next bent over in a burst of giggling, to Apple's delight. He looked around again to share his appreciation of this human touch with Mona. She began on a yawn. Reflecting vaguely that it was a pity she had to work so hard, Apple turned back the other way.

"Maria Sola," the woman said, coming off the stairs with a wide smile. Her dress was a sleeveless green tunic split up high on the thigh.

"Arnold Barker," Apple said, thinking that she was five feet ten if she was an inch.

"You must be a North American. You are so very tall." Her English had a strong accent.

For Apple, the rest was confusion for a while. He didn't know if one minute passed or ten. He did have the idea that he gave a shortened version of his cover story and mentioned that he was an inch over two metres tall. He did know that a first-name basis was rapidly reached. He did hear that Maria worked in nightclubs and was here hoping to get an engagement.

Clarity came with Mona asking, "How about breakfast, Miss Sola?" She was still standing across the lobby.

"But you must call me Maria also, please."

"Thank you. But one tries to maintain a proper relationship with the guests."

A friendly laugh, and "You English assassinate me."

"How charming," Mona said. "Pity I'm Welsh. Which, of course, doesn't answer the question of breakfast."

Maria smiled prettily. "Thank you, no. Eating before eleven in the morning is barbaric. I will take some coffee, however, if it is Spanish."

"Certainly, Miss Sola. This way. In the bar. That's where we keep our Italian espresso machine."

Apple wasn't sure if he took Maria's arm or if she took his. Whichever, he found himself going with her into the bar and there sitting beside her at a table. He thought: I'm smitten.

Maria began to speak. She had to break off because of the loud shriek of steam from the coffee machine, which Mona was tending behind the counter.

Apple got out his cigarettes. Hurt because they were bent from the packet being in his jeans hip pocket, he offered one to Maria. She took it with enthusiasm, as if it were something rare. Feeling a secret delight, Apple mused that she probably considered him to be quite a character.

He lit their cigarettes and the machine fell silent. Maria said, "I am surprised, Arnold, that you are not a policeman. You possess the tallness."

Apple nodded. He was having trouble in keeping his eyes from the tops of Maria's thighs, where he could see a hint of black panties with lacy edges.

"Perhaps you were a policeman once and gave it up to make more money, mm?"

"No, Maria, I've never been in the police. In fact, I have an idea that I'm *too* tall. They have limits either way."

"Then you could, I suppose, have become a private eye-ball."

Mona brought two coffees. "If there's nothing else," she said, "I'll go back and lounge around the kitchen."

Ignoring her, Maria started to talk about a detective series on television. She leaned closer, which meant having to turn so that her knees were pointing in the opposite direction. Apple gave a sigh.

"Something is wrong, Arnold?"

He nodded. "I'm envious of the way you speak another

language. Where did you learn your English?" He was pleased both with his fast, professional response and the fact that he hadn't lost touch completely with the operation.

They were still talking of schools a quarter hour later when Harry Lewis came in. He and the new guest, Apple gathered, had already met upstairs during a race for the bathroom.

"Maria, how about joining me in a brandy?" Harry asked, circling the bar.

"At this time of the day?" she said. "How disgraceful. Yes, please."

Apple frowned at the American for having stolen his thunder, toned down his quite-a-character status. He said, "I always think champagne is best for early mornings."

"Arnold, it doesn't go with coffee. No way. You want a shot of brandy?"

"No, thank you," Apple said, avoiding Maria's eyes.

Through from the patio, faintly, came the sound of the parrot squawking, "Dope."

Maria said, "We were talking, Harry, about Arnold being a policeman."

Harry looked up from pouring. "Oh?"

Apple and Maria both began to explain at the same time. So obviously was Maria pleased to be showing off her English that Apple let her take over. He looked through the partly open glass doors when once again Perky called, "Dope."

Crossing the lobby was white-clad Jason Lock. He moved oddly, delicately, like someone wearing spectacles for the first time, the impression heightened by his keeping his gaze rigidly ahead. It was as if, afraid of being seen, he wanted to creep, but was more afraid of being seen creeping.

Apple looked away as Harry Lewis came to the table. After putting down two glasses, he sat in a direct line with Maria's knees and said, "This reminds me of the last time I was in Hollywood."

Apple would have turned away in any case, out of disgust at the corny line being shot. He saw that Jason Lock was just going from sight, toward the front door. There was a suggestion more of the chicken-like creep in his gait.

Apple got up. Neither of the other two noticed. Maria was intent on the talk of Hollywood while Harry was flicking his gaze up and repeatedly down.

After waiting until he saw a Panama hat go by the window, Apple left the bar.

Hippie's attention was focussed along the street, in the direction taken by Jason Lock. Apple slipped outside and went the other way, bending at the knees and with his head lowered. Turning the first corner, he straightened and quickened his step. The next corner brought him within view of the ex-dentist.

Lock was walking in a normal manner now. Apple followed. He was led through the winding streets, around a covered market with its sick-sweet smell of fruit, and onto the main street, which was like an elongated square, a broad walkway in the middle. Apple began to feel that he could be wasting his time.

He wondered about Maria Sola. Was she what she gorgeously seemed, or was she there for his benefit, a trinket to divert him from his purpose? He would have to try to find out.

Jason Lock had stopped on the walkway to browse at a newsstand. Apple dropped to one knee and fiddled with a shoelace. Despite not having high hopes of this outing proving to be of value, he was enjoying himself.

The Englishman moved on. Ten minutes later he stopped

again, now at a bus stop. Others were waiting there also, some with children. By the paraphernalia it was evident that they were bound for the beach.

Apple turned back. He began to hurry when he saw a bus approaching. Musing that Jason Lock's timing was perfect, he strode to a taxi rank.

The driver of the first cab shook his head: he was eating a sandwich. The next was asleep, his cap tilted down. The third, he nodded an unenthusiastic agreement to the hire.

In the back, Apple asked, "Do you speak English?"

"Enough. Where you go?"

Apple pointed to the distant bus, which was moving on from having picked up the waiting people, the ex-dentist included. He said, "Follow that."

It was a long ride. The stops seemed to come every hundred yards, and the cabbie sighed at each one, as if he ached to go roaring past the bus. He brightened when, Jason Lock alighting, his passenger said, "Okay."

Apple took his time about getting out and paying. He moved on with the Englishman well ahead, his white hat showing among the sauntering crowd.

The beach was packed. That was the first thing Apple noted, with pleasure: his cover need was well supplied. What he noted secondly was so pleasurable/surprising that he was brought to a rocking halt.

Whichever way he looked, every woman was topless. From child to matron, the females wore only bikini bottoms. In all directions, at all levels, breasts ranging in size from golfball to melon swung and swooped, jazzed and jiggled.

Apple was in his element. He only wished he had the courage to stare, instead of taking fast, sneaky glances. But in any case, every time his eyes made their shy dart away, they met another naked bosom.

Hands afted, smiling on his top teeth, Apple ambled. He

let his gratified eyes wander, rest, roam, and hover, once he became less diffident through familiarity with the scene. He twiddled his fingers.

Apple hadn't been so happy in months.

For the second time today, he lost contact with the procession of minutes. He had no idea how many had passed when he at last came out of his trance.

This happened as Apple felt a prickling on his left arm and the left side of his face. For a moment he had the insane impression that half of him was blushing.

Then he realized that his skin was soaking up the sun. He was directly in its rays, which were strengthened by the nearby body of water. Apple glanced up worriedly.

With his fair skin, he had never been able to take strong sunshine. Even the British variety was damaging. A little brought him out in a rash, an average amount caused him to burn, a lot could put him in bed.

Apple started to hurry through the crowd. He circled the upright, strode over the prone. What he needed to do was both get out of the sun and find Jason Lock.

Apple tripped on a leg. He went sprawling. Losing his balance, he finished up on his hands and knees. On recovering from the fall he saw, several inches away from his face, a large pink nipple.

A woman's voice asked in German, "What is this?"

Apple, drawing back slightly, saw the whole breast, its sand-speckled mate, and then the woman's face. She was his own age and white-blond. She asked her question again, now in a far louder voice.

From all around grew a silence. Apple hissed, "Sorry." He got up and moved away, in a crouch, his eyes on the sand. He felt like the bumbling amateur whom he frequently suspected himself of being.

After circling a French family group—daughters bare,

mother naked—Apple straightened until he was able to see over heads. With the first broad sweep of his gaze he picked out the Panama hat. He headed in that direction.

Apple changed tack on seeing shelter. To his right, a small island of masts in a sea of humans, was a jumble of wind surfers. Signs said they were for rent. Some had their sails up, offering triangular patches of shade. There were few takers.

Apart from a girl at the triangle's tip, Apple had the shade to himself as he sank to a squat in the sand. Settled, cool, he looked around him at the protuberant scenery between glances at Jason Lock.

The ex-dentist was sitting among a stretch of sunbathing women. He sat placid, unmoving. He might have been alone, except that the attitude of his head suggested awareness, as well as contentment.

He's only here for the leer, Apple thought with a passing disappointment. He's a dirty old man—and long may the scorned breed prosper.

Apple's glances to Lock became fewer as his own eyes made careful choices, savoured, studied form. Unnoticed in the shade, he was able to stare without interruption. He wondered what Maria Sola would look like stripped to the waist.

Presently, Apple yawned. He'd had a disturbed night, he reminded himself, and that sun-scorching hadn't been any help. He ought to get on his way and leave the Englishman to his secret hobby.

Apple was about to get up when he heard a short swooshing sound. The next second, two things happened: the sail of the wind surfer came down on top of him, and the girl at the triangle's tip gave a sharp cry of pain.

Apple turned toward her, crawling at a push under the

floppy sail. Its mast, he realized, had hit the girl, who was sitting in a huddle with her hands to her head.

Others arrived there first, bending over the girl and pushing up the mast. A crowd was gathering, jabbering in half a dozen languages. All were asking what had happened. Someone said that the prop must have slipped in the sand, bringing the wind surfer off its mini-keel.

Although there was blood on her brow, the girl seemed to be all right, more shocked than physically damaged. Rising to his full height, Apple saw that Jason Lock was coming. He shrank again and slipped away through the people, not walking normally until he was well clear of the area.

Near the edge of the beach, Apple stopped. His prurient interest had been pricked. Sitting nearby was a buxom woman in a saggy straw hat. She wore a shirt that was held in the middle by one button. There was a full, generous spread of cleavage, which almost revealed the nipples.

Apple stared on. He was unconscious of shuffling closer—until the woman looked up, letting her face be seen from under the hat's brim. She was the same snub-nosed German as before. Her spine straightened abruptly.

Apple turned and hurried off.

Half an hour later Apple came out of a suburban car-rental agency. As in the other two he had just tried, there were no black cars for hire. He returned to the shop he had passed firmly some minutes before.

The window held clothing and notions. Apple saw only two items. One was a long brown wig. The other was a poncho with horizontal stripes of black and yellow. Awful mess, Apple thought, smiling nervously.

He reminded himself, however, that with the atrocious

pair he could avoid sunburn. The garment would cover him from the neck down; the rest would be taken care of by the wig, far more efficiently than would a hat, and he would rather say a good word for Angus Watkin than be seen in any kind of height-increasing headgear.

While busily reminding himself of the pair's usefulness as sun guards, Apple was ignoring the fact that since leaving the beach he had been constantly in the shadows of buildings.

He went into the shop.

Five minutes later, his pulses tapping, Apple came out wearing the poncho and the wig. Both tickled, but he didn't notice. He strode along with arms swinging and head high. He was elated. He had a feeling which he thought might be a sense of freedom. He would not, at this moment, have traded places with anyone in the world.

Apple was heading for another rental agency—having culled addresses from the telephone directory—when he saw the black car.

Out of automatic habit he had been looking at every black vehicle that appeared. What made him give this car closer attention was his having recognized the driver.

About to turn away, hide his face, Apple held on, remembering that he was as good as disguised. He allowed the car to pass within mere feet of where he stood.

Mrs. Arkwright was an awkward driver. She went along in fits and starts, mostly riding the clutch. To everything in her way she gave wide berth. She had blown the horn three times before reaching the end of the short street.

Which is when Apple began to follow. Running at a lope, he mused that, although the car was a Seat, and black, there was no other way to say it was the car he had been looking for. There was no way to say it wasn't, either.

At the corner, Apple saw that the Seat was still in view, zagging and spurting. He ran.

He ran along street after street. Sometimes he had to go at full pelt in order to keep the car in sight, what with Mrs. Arkwright speeding up on clear, straight stretches; sometimes he was able to go at a jog.

Apple sweated. Water came out to trickle all over his body. The ends of his wig stuck to his neck and cheeks. He was aware of every slimy tickle.

When the car came to a halt, Apple gasped with relief. He slowed to a dawdle. After drying his hands on the poncho, he got out a bent cigarette and lit up hungrily. It was a further help that he was in shadow, on the same side of the suburban street as the car.

Mrs. Arkwright had made no move to get out, though the lack of exhaust fumes showed that the motor was off. She appeared to be reading a book.

Apple went close. He told himself it had been a clever move of his, fitting himself up with a disguise. When level with the rear end of the car, he went to the wall and sank down into a cross-legged sit—Mrs. Arkwright the while glancing around briefly from her paperback.

Nothing else happened. The Englishwoman read, Apple sat. He was enjoying himself. The situation intrigued him, his get-up was a pleasure, pedestrians who spared him a look showed many types of response but never condescension.

A bus came, unloaded, left. It was seeing among the alighters many who had obviously been to the beach that caused Apple to give closer attention to his surroundings. He noticed now that he had been in this area earlier.

So it was less of a surprise when, after another half an hour of nothing happening, the ex-dentist came into view.

He walked straight to the car and opened the front passenger door with a mild flourish.

Mrs. Arkwright put her book down. "You were rather a long time, Mr. Lock."

"Couldn't be helped." He got in and closed the door. Its window was down. Apple could hear with clarity.

"He did follow you, I take it."

"He did, Mrs. Arkwright, yes. And I would say that he made a professional job of it."

"That's interesting." She started the motor. "I want to know all the details."

"Of course," Jason Lock said. "I wonder if anyone's mentioned the sandstone quarry to him yet."

What the Englishwoman answered was fogged by her gunning the motor. The car moved away in a series of jerks.

Apple sat on. He tried to make some kind of sinister sense out of what he had heard, in addition to absorbing the fact that he had been led on a dance by Jason Lock. What did it all mean?

Musing cheerfully, Apple got up at length and went on. He visited the last two car-rental agencies, had a sandwich lunch at a sidewalk café so that he could stay away from the pension (meaning wear his outfit) for as long as possible, strolled where it was shady, and in general had an extended wallow in his changed appearance.

Apple felt regret when in time he drew close to the old part of town. He took off his treasures. The wig he wrapped in the poncho, making a tight bundle. His walk became normal, holding less essence of stride.

At the Royal Rose, Mona was mopping the lobby floor. "Hello," she said, stopping work and touching the name brooch. "Been out shopping, Arnold?"

"Yes. The presents-from the people expect."

"For girlfriends, I suppose."

"No, a couple of aunts who might leave me a fortune."

They joked about dead man's shoes. Mona wiped her brow with the brush end of one of her plaits. She started mopping the floor again when Apple asked if Maria Sola was anywhere around.

"I really couldn't say, Arnold."

"Did she reserve in advance, by the way, or simply show up in the middle of the night, a stranger?"

"The second, like a witch on a broomstick."

"So you've never met her before?"

"No," Mona said. "After I've finished this chore, what say we sneak in the kitchen for a cupper tea?"

"Right. But what say I finish this chore for you?"

"Oh no, Arnold. I couldn't possibly let you."

When Apple had completed the mopping, he joined Mona, who had gone ahead to prepare the tea. They had a cosy chat. Apple told about overhearing some tourists mention a sandstone quarry.

"Is it worth seeing?"

For a moment, Mona looked blank. Then she said, "It's hardly a tourist attraction. An eerie place, actually. I don't know what he found so interesting about it."

"He?"

"George Trent. A guest who did a bunk without paying his bill. He said he went there a lot."

"Might be fun to have a look at it. How do I get there?"

"It's on the outskirts of town," Mona said. "One of these days, when I've got a moment to myself, I'll play guide."

Apple said, "That's a date." He changed the subject.

Later, up in his room, he opened his knapsack to put in the wig and the refolded poncho. At the bottom he saw a piece of paper. He brought it out. Both sides held a list of names.

Some seconds passed before Apple realized he had the missing page from the register.

"Dope," the parrot said. It swayed belligerently on its perch like a high diver threatening to be impressive.

No one took any notice. The four diners, at separate tables, went on eating their soup. There was no talk. It had been silent ever since Mrs. Arkwright had arrived and said, "We're dining in the patio again, I see. As it couldn't possibly be on account of the new guest, it can only be for someone else." She bowed at Apple in passing: "Good evening, young man."

Until Mona brought the soup, everyone had straightened cutlery, been fascinated by the tablecloth, listened avidly to clinks from the kitchen. Whenever a particularly loud sound had come from pots and pans, nods and shrewd glances had been exchanged. A major event had been Jason Lock opening out and lifting his newspaper.

Apple spooned up the last of his soup. He was still intrigued by the matter of the appearing ledger page. What it signified he didn't know. But he hoped to learn something from having passed the page on.

Following careful thought, and deciding against the main gambit of returning the page to its place in the register, Apple had gone to Jason Lock's room—the number of which, conveniently, he was given by the page itself. From the room he had heard the gentle snores of siesta, a plaintive lament in dead-march time. Quietly, he had slid the piece of paper under the door.

Everyone looked around at the clatter of high heels on tiles. Into the patio swept Maria Sola. She wore a tight skirt which had slits climbing almost to the hip bone, a skinny sweater, and a beret. From around her neck floated a yellow feather boa. She made a good entrance.

Apple and Harry Lewis both rose, both bowed, both performed furtive, one-handed gestures of invitation toward the vacant chairs at their tables, both curled their lips in callous smiles when Maria took a table by herself.

With the exception of Jason Lock, hidden behind his newspaper, the separate diners began on a stilted conversation. Maria was the focus. Apple got her attention part of the time by telling her about the farce his village amateur group had put on in the church hall last spring.

Mona started to bring the main course of rabbit stew with dumplings. Serving Apple last, she stood on to talk, resting her hip against the table. Politely, Apple looked around her toward Maria only once.

"When my chores are over," Mona said, "I'm going up to my room and indulge myself—in relaxation."

"That's the most sensible thing I've heard today."

"They're showing an old Garbo movie on television. Dubbed in Spanish, of course, but I know enough to get the gist. Do you like old movies, Arnold?"

"Absolutely," Apple said. He was forking open a dumpling while trying to hear what Maria was saying to Mrs. Arkwright. "The old ones are best."

"I'll slip into something comfortable," Mona said dreamily, gazing into space and tapping the ends of her plaits together. "I'll put the lights low and sprawl on the couch. Maybe I'll open a nice chill bottle of rosé."

Apple said warmly, concludingly, "That sounds marvellous."

Mona smiled. "Yes. Better than killing myself at the roller-disco. But I mustn't disturb you at the moment, must I? Eat well. I'll see you later." She left.

Apple got back into the four-way conversation and admired Maria's tight sweater while gently chewing dumplings. He gave the Spanish girl ten out of ten in every department. Admiring the way she threw a piece of bread at the parrot when it called out, "Brothel fodder," he couldn't stop himself applauding.

Maria turned to him with a wink. She tossed down her napkin, got up, and came across. Before Apple had a chance to make even a token rise, she had slid sensuously into the chair opposite.

"That is enough food," she said. "I must watch my figure."

Apple knew a clever comeback to that one but he couldn't think of it right now. He said, "Your figure's perfect."

"Exercise helps. I shall try the roller-disco sometime. What were you saying about a play in London?"

While Apple was telling of the *Hamlet* he and his friends had put on in the cathedral, Mona appeared. She was carrying a sandwich on a plate. After coming to a stop in the middle of the patio, she turned and went out again. Apple mused that, with all the work she had to do, it was hardly surprising that Mona got the orders confused.

"That's terribly interesting," Maria Sola said. "But I must admit that Mr. Shakespeare is too dull for me."

"It was a musical version."

Up to the table ambled Harry Lewis. He raised and dropped his sunglasses briefly, as though tipping a hat. "Arnold," he said. "Excuse me if I remind Maria that we have a date for an after-dinner brandy."

"I have not forgotten," Maria said, getting up. "Maybe Arnold would like—"

The American cut in, "No no, Arnold don't go for that kinda stuff. He's probably going to the roller-disco or something." He drew Maria away from the table. "Let's not let that brandy of ours get cold."

Hardly had the pair left the patio when Mrs. Arkwright came stumping along, her cane attacking the tiles. Halting nearby, she lifted her chin and asked, "Had a pleasant day, young man?"

"Yes, thank you," Apple said, folding his arms comfortably. "Shall I tell you what I did?"

"If you wish, of course."

He raised his voice. "First of all, I followed Mr. Lock. We'd had a chat the evening before about filling in time, and I was curious to see how he would spend his morning." With the Englishwoman looking at him balefully, he went on to tell of the beach, a long walk, and a meal out.

"I am delighted," Mrs. Arkwright said in a dead voice, "that you seem to be enjoying your holiday from—from whatever it is that you do."

"Husbandry."

"*Está un mosquito en tu mano.*"

If it had been smoothly done, in rapid Castilian with no broken accent, Apple might have fallen for the trick at least to the extent of glancing involuntarily at his hand, in search of the insect.

He frowned. "What was that, ma'am?"

"A Spanish expression," Mrs. Arkwright said. "Something along the lines of one swallow not making a summer." She turned away, her yellow eyes heavy. "Good night, Mr. Barker."

"And a very good night to you, Mrs. Arkwright."

When the thud-click had faded, Apple looked toward the last occupied table, from which he fully expected a visit, in keeping with all the others. Jason Lock stayed behind his newspaper. Apple got up, went over, brought the newsprint guard down with "Thank you, Mr. Lock, for showing me the way to that topless beach today."

The ex-dentist craned up a steady, placid gaze. He said, "I have no idea what you are talking about, Mr. Barker."

"It doesn't matter. What's of more moment, Mr. Lock, is

that today I got to thinking about George Trent. The name did strike a distant bell, so I looked in the registration book to see whereabouts in Britain he was from. And guess what?"

"I can't possibly."

Apple nodded gravely. "The page that has his name on it, it's been ripped out."

Jason Lock looked down. Carefully he folded his newspaper. "That," he said, "is most curious. But possibly a mistake on somebody's part."

"Wouldn't you agree that the plot, Mr. Lock, thickens?"

"Perhaps. One can never tell."

"Maybe I'm being melodramatic," Apple said, disappointed, and irked at being forced to admire the older man's cool. He switched to "I wonder if you could tell me what the roller-disco is, please."

"Gladly," the ex-dentist said. "And it's odd that you should ask. George Trent went there quite a lot."

Up in his room, having gone there to get a sweater, Apple first looked in his knapsack to see if the ledger page had been returned. It had not. Still kneeling, he wondered if Jason Lock would keep it, or pass it on to someone else; wondered, further, where the Englishman stood in all this, along with Mrs. Arkwright, and if everyone here wasn't part of the game.

Finding no answers, Apple got up and turned. He saw that on the pillow of his newly made bed there lay a rose. He shrugged. He supposed that it belonged to Mona or Martha, that one or the other had been wearing it in her hair and it had fallen out while she was making the bed.

After putting on a cardigan, Apple picked up the red flower, left the room, and went down to the lobby. It was deserted. Voices were coming from the bar. Apple put the rose with its mates in the vase and went out to the lamplit street.

He had gone several yards before realizing that he hadn't given a thought to Hippie: out of sight, out of mind: there had been an intervening line of traffic.

Now, rather than wait for that feeling across his back, or its absence, to tell him whether or not he was being followed, Apple glanced aside.

The shape in the corner of his vision was familiar. Hippie had come out of his doorway across the street and was tagging on behind.

Apple raised his arm. He hoped it would look like the slightly tardy movement that went with the head-turning; look as if he were checking his watch. It had never quite come off, or so the instructor said, when he had worked at the ploy in Training Four.

Apple dropped his arm and stopped. After giving a stupid-me shake of his head, he turned and started back.

Hippie was good. He kept on in the same direction and didn't even break step. Nor had he changed when Apple sneaked a look while turning into the pension.

In his room, his cardigan off, Apple collected the poncho and wig. He held the bundle behind him as he went downstairs. Through the bar's glass doors he could see Maria and Harry, with Martha behind the counter polishing a glass.

Feeling like Jason Lock, Apple went cautiously across the lobby. He reached the door safely and slipped on his sun guard/disguise/alter ego. He waited for the cover of traffic before going out. He didn't bother to look for Hippie, who, in any case, was quickly forgotten because of Apple's discovery.

He could make himself smaller. The poncho having a low hem, he was able to bend at the knees without that act being observable.

Apple was thrilled. He felt tall only in spirit. Through the wig's dangling strands he looked at himself in every shop window that he passed. He tried different heights, rising and sinking gracefully as he walked, and settled on the one that gave least trouble to his thighs and spine.

An even six feet, Apple reckoned in delight. He ignored what the window reflections told him other than size: that his knees prodded awkwardly at the poncho's front, his buttocks poked it out at the back. He was smaller. His alter ego bloomed.

For an hour Apple walked along the brightest, busiest streets, with occasional halts to rest his back and bent legs. He noted with pleasure the glances of admiration from weirdly dressed girls, the looks of envy from sober-dressed men. Store windows were a constant treat.

For longer periods Apple tried out other heights. He had a spell of being five feet five inches tall, and thought it had quite a lot going for it. He was Mr. Average at five-nine for a while, and felt that it had a definite charm. He tried to get down to five feet, but trod on the poncho's hem and tripped up.

That, normally, would have produced a bout of furious blushing. Apple was protected by the outfit and his thriving alter ego. He even glared haughtily at a passer-by who sniggered.

Finally, arrogant and sated, Apple set off to find the discotheque which Jason Lock had told him about, where the dancing was done on roller skates.

The foyer was crowded. Staff were dour natives. Customers, tourists, and foreign-colony members, the plain or colourful birds of short or long passage. Most people were sitting on stools, putting on roller skates.

Apple was handed a pair in exchange for his entrance fee. Wheels, frame, and straps were all of the same orange plastic, which was scarred ugly with use.

Still in his semi-squat, Apple went to a stool. Skates quickly strapped on, he rose and moved cautiously toward an arch that led to the disco proper. His attention was directed mainly downward as he worked at reminding his muscles of the skill they used to have, some fifteen years ago, in the art of skating.

He entered a large, low-ceilinged room. It was trembling to the boom of hard rock, echoing to the crash of skates, disappearing every third second as the strobe lights flashed completely out instead of their continual midway dip. Skater-dancers were everywhere; some carefully circling the floor's edges, most cavorting in the middle.

Moving with fair ability, Apple skated in and out of dancers, his poncho billowing. After a moment, he was surprised to realize that his feeling of well-being had vanished. It was as though he had left it outside on the street. Another minute passed before he understood the problem.

His head almost touched the ceiling. He was unable to crouch on the skates, the skates themselves added four inches to his height, another inch was added by the wig. He had become at least seven feet tall. People were either looking at him oddly or, grinning, were giving him the freak treatment.

Apple headed for the apron of the floor. There, beyond a handrail, were couches and tables. He would sit down or leave. He wasn't sure why he had come here in the first place. Apart from everything else, the lights and music were an attack on his senses.

In his haste to leave the dancers, Apple went too fast. He collided with a girl. They held each other up with a partial embrace. Apple shook his head in disbelief on seeing that the girl was the blonde he had met twice on the beach that morning.

With a frown, she reached up and flipped aside his curtain of hair. In German she accused, "But it is you again."

"I'm sorry if I—" he began, unthinkingly in the same language. After breaking off he turned away and skated on.

Reaching the handrail, Apple saw Martha March. She was further around on the apron, leaving a stretch of counter carrying drinks on a tray.

Apple stayed on the floor to move in that direction. He was glad of the diversion, glad of the noise and flashing lights: they stopped him from berating himself over the language slip.

He came opposite to where Martha sat. At the table with her were Harry Lewis and Maria. As they all saw him, as he pulled his wig-curtain back, Maria jumped up, came to the rail, and vaulted it with a flashing display of upper thighs.

It was too noisy to hear the crash as her skates hit the floor, and Apple only just caught her eager "We will dance."

He shouted, "I think I'd rather sit down."

"You do not like dancing?"

"Yes, but I'm tired. I've already been dancing for a long time."

"Nonsense, Arnold. Come along." She grabbed him and spun them both into a twirl. "I love your outfit."

Which should have stayed a disguise, Apple told himself. He was doing everything wrong.

By now they were in the middle of the floor; and by now Apple's spiritual discomfort had been joined by the physical. Under the wig and poncho he was sweating profusely.

"Sorry," he yelled. "I'm too tired."

Maria mouthed, "It must be catching. You are not going to faint, are you?"

"I don't know what you mean."

Maria moved in close to perform the nightclub shuffle. At least, Apple thought, the relationship in their heights had stayed the same because of her own skates.

Maria said, "Tonight, just before I left the pension, Mona fainted."

"Really? What happened to her?"

"No idea, Arnold. She was standing at the reception desk, alone, and suddenly she collapsed. Martha and myself, we saw her up to bed."

"She works too hard."

"Possibly," Maria said. "Anyway, she did not do her person any damage, falling. She only broke a vase of flowers."

"That's something."

Maria pushed herself away and grinned playfully. "Catch me, Arnold!" she shouted. She swung aside and skated off with long strides.

Apple would have liked to be able to oblige, but simply wasn't up to it. He was turning to make his way over to the apron when the jolt came in his back.

It sent him into a wheeled stagger. He went zooming across the floor with his arms fighting for balance, though they were hampered in this by the poncho. He sideswiped one dancer, bounced off another. Behind him he left shouts that were angry-loud enough to be heard above the booming music.

Apple came to the rail. He was able to stay upright. But before he was totally recovered, he felt another jolt push on his shoulder.

As the force shot him away, he managed a fast glance

back. He saw a tall, thickly built man who was dressed like a tourist, except for being hooded with a wig.

The other way, across the floor, stood a man of the same style. By his posture and the way he was watching, Apple guessed him to have been the author of the first shove. He wondered if this was some kind of game peculiar to the disco. Except that there had been nothing friendly about those jolts.

By grabbing a dancer who was a novice on skates, Apple ended his unplanned trip. He changed direction, coasted toward the side. Before he reached it, a third like-dressed man had appeared abruptly on his right, coming straight for him at skillful speed.

Their shoulders smashed together. Apple, the recipient, went flying sideways. This time he fell. Even though he landed with a certain amount of professionalism, rolling, there were still trills of pain in his elbows and knees. And the skate of a passing dancer clumped against his ankle.

Apple rose swiftly. One of the men, or yet another of the same tourist-resident composition, was skating toward him with head set forward. Clearance in the wig showed a determined mouth.

Although Apple didn't know what it all meant, he felt sure it was no game. He waited until the man was almost on him, then shot down to a foetal crouch.

With a yell, the man went toppling over his back.

Up again, Apple circled the floor's centre area. He didn't try to pinpoint his friends from the pension. Against three or more men, two girls and a middle-aged man wouldn't be a lot of help.

What Apple did see, in the moment when the lights went black, was a red sign indicating the way to an emergency exit.

He aimed himself that way, making a fast swerve when one of the attackers came charging at him.

He shot through a gap in the rails.

Apple slipped around couches, tables. The wheels of his skates came ditheringly onto rippled concrete. It was the surface of a ramp, going down. In the dim but steady glow of a red light, Apple descended swiftly to a pair of doors. They were held shut by a crush bar.

Knowing that such devices were noted more for their success at keeping out interlopers than for releasing the endangered, Apple stopped breathing while he pushed on the bar of metal. He gasped in air as the doors opened.

Skating outside, Apple found himself in a passageway, a mere slice of space between buildings. It was three feet across. The walls on either side were whitewashed and without breaks.

Apple heard the doors crash behind him as he went on. The swinging use of his arms being impossible in the confined space of the passage, he pulled himself along by using his hands on the walls. At least, he thought, this is keeping the bastards in single file.

Apple was afraid. That, he told himself, was because the unknown was always frightening. The men formed a mystery. He didn't know what they wanted, who they were, or what they intended. For all he was aware, this could still be part of a game.

Continuing to sweat on account of his efforts, Apple wall-paddled along to the end of the passageway. He came out into an alley. It was dim and deserted. He repeatedly dipped his body to the task of skating at speed.

Looking back on a bend, he saw the three men pop one

behind the other from the passage's mouth. One had lost his wig. His hair was cropped short and seemed un-Spanishly fair. He quickly took the lead from his friends.

Apple skated as fast as he dared without risking a fall. It was nowhere near as fast as the speeds he used to reach. He knew that his best hope for safety was in numbers: that he would soon come to where there were people.

The alley widened out. It became a street, though one that was as narrow as all the thoroughfares in the old part of town. It weaved like a discarded piece of string. The houses were shuttered, the business places were closed, there were no people about. The only sound came from the small plastic wheels.

Looking back again, Apple saw that the leader was mere yards behind, with the other pair about the same distance to his rear. Beyond that came another figure. Sex was impossible to discern. Also unknown was whether the fourth chaser was friend or foe.

Two men appeared from a doorway. Apple slowed, but then changed his mind. He began to speed up again. The slow-up, however, had lost him most of his lead. He could hear the first pair of roller skates right at his back.

Apple went around another bend. He seemed to be going as slowly as in a nightmare. The poncho was a real hindrance to the work his arms needed to do. And next, he felt the tail of the poncho grabbed.

He was jerked backwards, almost to a stop. His body and that of the leader collided. Apple twisted sideways. He jabbed back with his elbow. It made perfect, hard contact with the man's face. Blood shot from his nose.

Hold broken, the man fell back. He hit the pair behind. There was a general three-way grabbing to stay erect.

For another nightmarish few seconds, Apple found himself

unable to move from the spot, like a swimmer having difficulty in getting his stroke. He cursed the skates and wondered if he dare spare the valuable time to try and rip them off.

Then he was rolling forward, with the trio still struggling and the fourth person coming swiftly through the shadows. Apple would have looked closer except for seeing a passage. He went to it and inside—and realized at once that he had made a mistake.

Not unusually here, there were steps. Going down would have been tricky enough on skates; these steps were ascending. But it was too late to go back. And the single-file necessity would again be in his favour.

As Apple dropped to his hands and knees, he heard a clamour of wheels in the passage's mouth. He started crawling up the steps. Again his poncho proved a drawback. It got under his knees as well as his hands. He spared a precious moment to drag up the front and take it into his mouth.

A hand grabbed his ankle. He tried to shake free. He succeeded, went up two more steps, then felt his foot retaken, this time by two hands. By the snuffly wet breathing from behind he guessed the grabber to be the man with the bloody nose.

Apple gave a mighty heave away with his leg. He freed himself, leaving the skate behind, and his knee hit a step.

The poncho flew from his mouth as he yelped with pain. The yelp was still lasting when he began to rise. He leapt to his feet. The leg with the paining knee, it buckled on taking his weight. That made him fall against the wall.

The two hands took hold again, at ankle and calf. Apple had to put all his weight on the hurt leg in order to kick back with the other. His groan was covered by the cry that came when his skate struck home. The hands released him.

Using mostly his skateless foot, Apple went quickly up the steps. He was able to take them five or six at a time with his long stride. This was one of those rare times when he was glad of his height. He smiled at the sounds of clattery chase.

Steps and passage ended together. Apple came out onto a street. It was the one that held the handicraft market. Most of the stalls were down, but there were still many vendors and browsers around. Apple moved along between them at a casual speed, using the one skate as a scooter. He knew he was safe now.

Apple awoke early; too early for breakfast. Dressed in jeans and shirt, he went downstairs in the sleepy silence and let himself out. He was carrying a single roller skate in orange plastic.

All the doorways along the street were void of life. Apple began to walk. Humming idly, he went back over the possibilities in connection with last night's escapade.

First, the trio could be working for the same someone who had ordered the hit-and-run attempt and the scorpion. In which case, was that someone the fourth person on the chase? Either way, were orders coming from the KGB or from the *capo* of a local, or national, even international, gang of drug traffickers?

Second, the trio could have been drunken toughs with nothing better to do with their time.

Third, the object could have been robbery: mugging on wheels.

Fourth, the men were friends of the German woman whom he had seen at the beach and at the disco, and whom they thought he was dogging for some reason, maybe lustful.

Fifth, it could be a game.

Apple discounted the second, third, and fifth as unlikely.

First was his favourite, with the background figure being under the control of Moscow. But he still couldn't say whether the aim was to kill him, maim him, or simply scare him away. With everything being so heavy-handed, the last seemed the most feasible.

Apple stopped humming as he came to the street market, now an emptiness of litter. He quickened his step, frowning. On his turning into the passage, one ridge faded off the frown's collection: he hadn't been sure he would find the right place.

But he had, and now he also found what he was looking for. The rest of the frown ridges went as he trotted down the steps. Relieved that his guilt would go, that he would be able to return the disco's property, he picked up the roller skate that he had lost last night.

Apple went on down. Five minutes later he was leaving both skates by the closed front door of the disco. Another five, and he was walking into the pension.

A tinkling led Apple into the dining room. There, Martha was setting a table. After they had greeted one another, Apple asked, "How did you get on at the disco?"

"Good fun. You shouldn't have left so early."

Apple told of having seen a game that looked to be getting rough. Martha said she hadn't seen anything and asked what kind of game it had been. She shrugged to signal mystification when Apple described the opening action on the dance floor. Which, he thought, took care of the fifth possibility.

Sitting at the table, he said, "How's Mona this morning?"

"Oh, she's fine, but having a lie-in. So I've had to do the towels in addition to all my usual jobs."

"I wonder what caused her to faint?"

Martha gave that shrug again. "Search me."

Now it occurred to Apple that the New Zealander wasn't

her normal, brash self. In her attitude there was a hint of awkwardness. And, instead of bustling away as soon as the table had been laid, she stayed on to fiddle unnecessarily with the cutlery.

Apple was trying to remember, from Training Three, how you went about encouraging a confidence that its owner seemed to want to give, or be rid of, when the hefty girl said, "Look, Arnold, it's none of my business what you're up to. And maybe you're not up to anything—just being incognito. But I think I ought to tell you that I know."

Apple leaned back in his seat. He smiled faintly. "You know what, Martha?"

"What you really are. Your job."

He broadened the smile and shook his head, and hoped he was doing the act well. "I don't get it. Is it a joke?"

Martha also shook her head. "When I took a clean towel into your room," she said, putting a hand into her apron pocket, "I found this on the floor. You must've dropped it. Don't worry, I won't say anything to the others."

"I really don't . . ."

"Now excuse me. I'll get your breakfast." She left.

Apple leaned forward to look at what Martha had put on his place setting. It was a card coated in plastic. In one corner was a thumbprint, in another a photograph. The rest was writing: data: name, place, rank, height, colouring. They said, going backwards, fresh, six-seven, Detective Inspector, Scotland Yard, Arnold Barker. The face in the photograph belonged to Apple.

CHAPTER 3

For most of that same day, Apple loitered about the pension. He was both hoping for something to happen and trying to figure out what he thought of as the Yard Card. Neither came to fruition.

There were times when he experienced lethargy and a stultifying boredom. That was something he had never expected to feel while on a mission. He supposed, finally, that field work in espionage could have as many patches of tedium as its Upstairs variety. This view depressed him until he realized that it meant he was possibly becoming less of a romantic, therefore more of a pro. He roused himself from lethargy.

Apple tried to provoke either action or solution. He prowled the upstairs corridors, poked around below, wore a face of suspicion. All he succeeded in doing was discovering a back way out of the building, which he thought might come in useful.

Next he cornered each of his fellow guests in turn. They were less interested in giving answers than in asking questions of their own. He learned nothing, started nothing.

Mona, he saw briefly several times. She looked pale. The reason she had fainted, she said, must have been because of the diet she had gone on two or three days before. She had been overzealous in her ambition to become less plump.

"But why diet?" Apple asked. "I think you look great."

She blinked up at him. "Come on, Arnold. I'd give anything to have a body like Maria's."

"Have you seen her around, by the way?"

"No. Excuse me."

Apple saw Martha only in passing, not to talk to. That made it unnecessary for him to have to decide on what he was going to say to her about the Yard Card, or if he was going to say anything at all.

After siesta, Apple left by the rear exit. It fed to an alley, which led to a street. He went to the nearest car-rental agency and with his Arnold Barker credit card rented a yellow Citroën 2CV.

He drove to the topless beach, which might be a way, he told himself, to provoke some action.

The late-afternoon sun was mellow, kind, the air cool. Apple was untroubled by thoughts of sunstroke as he wandered among the people. He felt lethargic without being bored.

Apple found a place to sit among the plethora of females. He looked about him while squeezing handfuls of sand. When the sun went behind a cloud, and shirts began to be donned, Apple turned his mind once again to the Yard Card.

He got the identification out, examined it, put it away again. He had learned no more than he had on all the previous examinations. The card looked genuine, though of course that could not be so, unless the bearer's name had been cleverly altered and the photograph exchanged.

That, the picture, had a bleakness that could mean it had been taken outdoors. But since a collar and tie were on show, it couldn't have been taken here in Ibiza, outdoors or in.

Apple went over the same questions. Had Martha really found it on the floor of his room, or was she pulling a neat one—for herself or somebody else? And what was the neat one anyway? Was the instigator saying: You may not be this exactly but you're up to something nosy? Was it, again, a warning?

Apple was glad when the sun came out. He went back to looking at the scenery and squeezing sand.

Presently, the grittiness on his palms made Apple think of sandstone, which reminded him of the quarry. He grinned in minor triumph. Getting up, he assured himself that he had known all along that there had been a reason for his coming out here to the beach.

He returned to the car, drove to the street behind the pension, parked there, and walked around the block. Approaching the Royal Rose, he saw that Hippie was in his doorway. It was the same man every time, Apple now knew, not a series of replacements, for by this time he had got a fix on Hippie's stance and physique.

Drawing level, Apple waved. The only response was a slight twitch of the Zapata moustache. Apple smiled, went on, and turned into the pension.

"Well, you look happy enough," Mrs. Arkwright said. She was standing bulkily in the lobby.

Apple halted. "With autumn weather like this—sure."

"I suppose it will be raining felines and canines where you come from in—um—?"

"I suppose exactly the same, ma'am."

The Englishwoman thumped her cane on the tiles. "You have been to the beach, I see, Mr. Barker."

While lifting a hand to feel if there was sun heat on his face, Apple wondered about that *Mr.* Had it been a shade stressed, as though to imply that another title would be more correct, maybe Detective Inspector?

"It's quite elementary," Mrs. Arkwright said. "There is sand on your footwear."

Apple looked down. Looking up again slowly, he said a casual "No, ma'am, that's not from the beach. As a matter of fact, I've been to the sandstone quarry."

Nothing seemed to change in the yellowy eyes, no muscle flinched behind the mask of cosmetics, no alien chord lit the voice for "To which quarry do you refer?"

Deflated, Apple said, "I didn't know there were lots."

"There are. Both abandoned and functioning. All totally void of interest as far as I'm concerned." She turned aside. "Pardon me if I rush away. Mr. Lock is waiting in the bar to be beaten at chess."

Apple went on. While checking out the dining room and then the kitchen, he told himself he was doing brilliantly. He tried to be wry about it.

Mona was in the patio, changing tablecloths. She looked around with a smile, her plaits swinging. "Hello, Arnold. Dinner won't be for an hour yet."

"I know. I came out here looking for you."

Mona paused over unfolding a cloth. "Really?"

"That's right," Apple said. He pulled free a nearby chair and sat on it in reverse. "I was thinking about how hard you work. Thinking that what you needed right now was a little break."

"Right now?"

"Yes. A spin in the country is exactly what the doctor would order—if you went to see one, which you should."

Bringing the tablecloth to her chest, Mona protested that she was perfectly fit, that she had dinner to think of, that in any case she couldn't take herself for a spin anywhere because she didn't have a car.

"Ah, but I have one," Apple said. "I rented it a little while ago."

"You rented . . . ?"

"So I, dear lady, will do the taking. If you're agreeable. And if you'll allow dinner to be late for once. Have you any more objections?"

Mona gazed around. Apparently she found "Where would we go?"

Apple got up. While replacing the chair neatly he said, "You could show me that sandstone quarry someone mentioned to me the other day. You know the one."

Mona put down the cloth and turned away. "I'll get a scarf."

Dusk was beginning as they came out of the alley. Apple said it was handy, being able to make a shortcut like this. Mona said she used the pension's back way so seldom that she had almost forgotten it was there. "How did you discover it, Arnold?"

"I was being nosy this morning to pass time."

"Not bored with your holiday already, I hope."

"Oh no. Quite the reverse. It's getting more and more interesting. Here's the car." He stepped ahead and opened the passenger door. "Your limousine, madame."

Mona got in. "Thank you, my good man."

They kept up the banter while driving out of town, through dull suburbs, past uninteresting countryside. Apple had no notion of what, if anything, he would accomplish by this outing, but felt somehow that it was a step in the right direction.

He and Mona fell silent after the yellow Citroën had turned off onto a dirt road. Apple needed to concentrate: the way was single-width, uneven and winding.

It grew worse, adding steepness to the other faults. Apple

had to engage first gear to chug up the narrow, twisting incline. He went even slower as a sheer incline developed on the right.

He said, "Don't look down."

"I thought that was for mountain climbers. Myself, heights don't bother me." She paused. "I mean, height itself does matter. It's important. I like tallness."

"Mmm," Apple mumbled, steering with care. He wondered if the outing was a mistake. "How far now?"

"No further. We're here."

They levelled out onto a plateau the size of twin tennis courts. The drop lay on three sides; the other was a continuing climb of land, steep, dotted with rocks and mapped by footpaths.

Apple and Mona went up one of the latter after leaving the car. There was a breeze. It whispered around them as they climbed at a zigzag. The distance showed a sprinkling of lights in the growing dusk. The way underfoot was dim.

Relievingly soon they came onto another, final plateau. It was much larger than the other. The uneven ground was scarred by rectangular holes, each walled slopingly with sandstone and descending to an untidy point. The impression was of the shell from which a small pyramid had been removed whole.

Scattering the surface were wild olive trees, as thin and bent as crones. Their meagre foliage moaned back a protest at the breeze, which had more strength up here.

Apple heard another sound. "Is that a car?" he asked, less from interest than to make human contact. He thought this place wild and weird, with an ambience akin to that of a graveyard.

"Probably," Mona said. "But it could be miles away. Up here sound carries."

"Not a very cheerful place."

"It's all right by daylight. Nice for picnics."

They began to wander between the odd-shaped pits, with Mona explaining how the workers used to cut out the building blocks with saws, tapering off when they reached rock.

Apple split from her to circle one of the holes. Its bottom, he saw, held a dark mass. He paused to peer downward. He had identified the mass as a collection of garbage when he began to overbalance. By a wheeling of his arms, he got his balance back.

Suddenly, Apple decided he had had enough. He didn't like this place. That the dislike might be irrational didn't trouble him. The quarry was oppressive.

He said firmly, "Okay, let's go."

"Seen enough? Well yes, I suppose you have. There's not much to it really. Come on, I'll race you back."

Mona darted away. Apple went after her with less speed, but felt pleasant about the act of leaving. Which feeling grew stronger as, walking now, Mona having gone from sight into victory, he reached the edge and began to make his way carefully down. He was whistling cheerily when he came onto the lower patch of level.

Mona was waiting in the heavy gloom. "Slow coach," she panted.

Apple went close to her. "You haven't had much of a spin. Shall we go somewhere else?"

"No, thanks. I must get back. And this is fine. I enjoyed it. I feel about sixteen years old."

"You look it," Apple said, bending to lessen the distance between them. "Seventeen at the most."

"Thank God for twilight and candlelight and the soft light of stars."

"That sounds like poetry."

Mona lowered her voice. "Don't tell me you're a poetry fan."

They talked for a minute of poets, agreeing over Keats and Wilfred Owen, disagreeing over Byron and Thomas. Mona said that likes and dislikes were funny things.

Apple nodded. After a moment of silence he said, "Would you mind if I asked you something?"

Mona eased closer, looking up. "Not at all, Arnold."

"Well, I don't know if I dare."

"Try. Please ask me."

Apple said, "I wouldn't want to offend you."

"You wouldn't," Mona said in a husky voice. "I promise I won't be. Ask me anything you like, Arnold."

Nodding again, deciding, Apple said, "I wonder if I could have some lemon marmalade with my breakfast toast?"

In the following quiet, Mona eased away, while Apple slowly tensed. He was glad of the poor visibility: his blush wouldn't be seen. He had been wrong, he realized in simmering anguish, to ask for an extra. Mona had enough to look after without worrying about unnecessary details.

Apple blurted into speech at the same moment as Mona. He repeated that it didn't matter about the marmalade flavour, orange was fine; she said she didn't know if she could get any of the lemon kind.

Mona stopped talking first. She turned and went toward the car. Apple followed, throwing ahead a final "It doesn't matter in the slightest."

Back in a silence, they entered the 2CV. Apple started the motor and switched on lights. The engine he revved up far more than was needful, wanting the noise.

He said loudly, "It's safe to reverse here, isn't it? There's no back-up light on this car."

Mona's voice was equally loud, her words clipped: "Quite

safe. There are rocks along the edge. Stop when you touch them with your wheels."

Apple began to reverse in the darkness. Though feeling like driving at speed, he went slowly, for which he was vastly relieved some seconds later, when he felt the rear wheel on Mona's side leave the plateau and spin into space.

Apple slammed his foot on the brake pedal. As the car jolted to a stop, he himself stopped, freezing all body movement. Even his eyes he kept perfectly motionless.

Mona asked, "What's wrong?"

Apple hissed, "Be quiet!"

When she spoke again it was in a whisper. "Why?"

A gust of breeze came along. It caused the car to rock gently, obliquely, corner to corner, and Mona to answer her own question with a choked "Oh."

"Exactly," Apple whispered, risking one fast glance from the corners of his eyes, during which he noted that Mona had become as statue-like as himself. He went on, explaining the understood:

"That corner of the car behind you is over the edge. The other back wheel is almost there, maybe right on the rim. One false move, one strong gust of wind—and over we go."

After the sound of swallowing, came "It's a hundred-foot drop down there. I'm terrified."

"Don't be," Apple said. By the tone of his whisper he knew that he was terrified as well. "Everything's going to be fine."

Mona hissed, "Keep your voice down."

Carefully, slowly, tensely, Apple took his right hand off the steering wheel and lowered it toward his knee. From near there he eased it into the darkness under the dashboard.

Working by touch, he found and clasped the handle of the parking brake. He kept his eyes on the headlight-whitened patch of ground ahead while creepingly pulling the brake on. As it clicked over the final notch, Mona made a wheezy noise that showed she had been holding her breath.

"Yes," Apple murmured, his body frozen again, "that's a bit better." He continued, soothingly, to ease his own fear as well as Mona's, "The parking brake on the 2CV is one of the best in the world."

"Oh?"

"It has to be, you see, to compensate for the fact that the gears are light. They alone wouldn't hold the car on a hill."

Breeze gusted by in a moan, as if complaining at how little damage it was doing. The yellow car, shuddering, tilted down at the back a short way and then came up level again.

It could only have been in an attempt to avoid the fact of danger that Mona whimpered, "What happened to the rocks?"

"Moved by kids, anyone."

"Don't speak so loudly."

"I'm not," Apple whispered as he began to ease the gear stick toward him, out of reverse. His foot had been down on the clutch since the same second that he had slammed the brake on. That pedal he still held firmly down, despite his confidence in the parking brake.

Easing the stick, he said, in a ploy similar to Mona's, "In fact, the gears on the 2CV are so weak you can't start these cars with motion—a tow or a push."

Mona breathed, "That's terribly interesting."

Apple drew on the stick gently but firmly. "In further fact, the Citroën 2CV is probably the only car nowadays that comes equipped with a starting handle."

"What a useful thing to know."

"Yes," Apple said, the word coming out like a long hiss as

he brought the gear stick into the neutral slot. He took several deep breaths.

Now, he thought, his mind being cold and pedantic. What next? Does one put it into first and try to pull ahead?—which is possible with front-wheel drive. Or does one try to get out of the car as it is? The first means one having to let the parking brake off. And what if one accidentally allowed the motor to stall?

"No," he mumbled.

Mona asked a faint "No what?"

He told her what they were going to do while letting out the clutch pedal. Both completed, he risked another arm movement to switch off the motor.

The complaint of the wind seemed louder in the new silence. Not allowing it to go on, Apple said, "Lean forward and in my direction. But slowly. Slowly." He demonstrated by sloping his torso at a forward angle. When the windshield, acting as a mirror, told him that Mona had done the same—he didn't turn his head—he reached for and got hold of the doorknob. His clasp was so gentle he might have been taking the hand of a sick child.

"Is it safe?" Mona whispered.

"No, but it's the saf*est*."

"I think I'm going to sneeze."

"If you do," Apple said, but left the rest unfinished. He didn't want to think about it. He didn't dare.

The knob snicked back smoothly. Leaning still further to his left, Apple touched his shoulder to the door. He pressed gently. Nothing happened. Beginning to apply more force, he heard a sound that he took at first to be a return of the breeze; then he realized that it was Mona spasmodically sucking in air.

Apple swiftly spun the index-card wheels in his mental store of odd information. He pounced on the anti-sneeze trick which needed least physical activity, gasping, "Pinch your nostrils while trying to blow out through your nose."

Mona obeyed, he saw via the reflection. He gave his attention back to the door.

With more pressure it creaked away from its frame. He went on arming it away, slowly, until it stood wide open. A pang of regret took him at the fact that, because of the passenger, he couldn't make an immediate escape by flinging himself out.

Mona panted, "I think I'm all right."

"Keep hold of your nostrils."

"Yes. Don't worry."

"And stay still till I give you the word."

She whispered, "I'm too afraid to move."

"You'll have to in a minute," Apple said. He increased his lean, aiming for the gaping doorway, at the same time gradually moving his legs around to that side of the seat.

Moaning came with the breeze. The car shuddered, rocked. Apple continued with his slow-motion changing of position. He was in a sideways sit by the time the moan faded.

Like a sleepwalker, Apple stretched his arms out. He took a two-handed grip on the door's top. Cautiously he drew himself outside, though keeping his feet on the floor of the car.

Soon he was standing, having gone from a crouch to fully erect. He shuffled, moving each foot an inch at a time, until he was by the doorframe's front.

After a pause to recover from the effort, Apple said, "All right now. Start moving this way. Very easy does it. And don't let go of your nose."

Even if he had twisted around he could not, from this position, have seen inside the car. It was just as well, he thought. Instead, he listened anxiously to each foot-scrape and spring-squeak and breath-gasp, sensed the fear, felt the brush of bodies as Mona eased herself behind him and through the doorway.

She jumped free. The car lurched. Apple flung himself away. He landed badly, fell and rolled. Droopy with relief, he sat up. The yellow 2CV was still there, rocking gently.

Mona came to him. "Are you all right?"

"Perfectly." He got up.

It seemed only natural that they should embrace. For two pins Apple would have kissed Mona on the brow. He made do with giving her shoulder a jolly good patting.

Stepping apart, Apple said, "So let's start footing it back to town. We might get a lift. You go to the pension, I'll see about a tow truck."

"I feel more like lying down than walking."

"It's mostly downhill. Come on."

After leaving the plateau, they became verbally animated, which Apple recognized as the infant form of shock. They vied with each other in the retelling of their adventure.

Because of the sharing of danger, Apple felt close to Mona. He felt he should express it, but didn't know how. He would have held her hand except that she might consider the act to be improper, too familiar.

Presently, talk easing, Apple said that he had never really cared for lemon marmalade. It was a habit.

Two hours later, Apple was parking the Citroën in the street behind the pension. He and Mona had been picked up soon after reaching the main road. The driver had taken

Mona on to town after dropping Apple off at an outskirts garage, where he had spent the longest part of the evening's affair in trying to explain the situation without daring to use any Spanish.

Finally, with drawings and mime, the message had been transmitted. Apple returned to the plateau with two mechanics in a breakdown truck.

The men were entertained by the situation. Good-naturedly, they referred to their customer as a long-legged English idiot, one who not only had left the headlights on but who could have driven clear of the edge by jamming rocks behind the front wheels to prevent any backward movement.

For that, Apple had been forced to agree with the idiot part, especially when it took the truck all of one minute to bring the car fully onto the level, and even further when, after he had paid and tipped, one man told the other, "If this nice, tallish fellow had telephoned the car-rental agency, they would've come and pulled him out for nothing."

The pension's back way led into the patio. As Apple entered, the parrot shrieked, "Dope!" That was followed by a clatter from the lobby of high heels on tiles. Next, through the double doors came Maria Sola.

The entertainer was stunning in a short bright red dress with a low V-neck, a girdle of white rope, and shiny red boots that rose to her knees. Breasts and black hair bounced as she strode to Apple as though she were about to berate him for some transgression.

He smiled uncertainly. "Good evening."

"It has not been so far," Maria said, folding her arms. "I am bored. I have been working my fingers bony while you have been having risqué adventures with our charming hostess."

"Risky," Apple said, "is the word."

"I wonder. But let it be. Mona told us of your escapade. She returned just after Martha and I and Mrs. Arkwright had finished preparing the dinner."

"That was nice of you all. What's on the menu?"

Maria shook her head. "Nothing. All finished. Harry and Mr. Lock are washing the dishes."

"I'm hungry," Apple complained. He was looking everywhere on the front of the red dress except at the cleavage.

"Good. Then we shall go for a bite. In your car. You should have told me before that you had a car."

"I got it only today, Maria. Would you really like to go out somewhere?"

The answer seemed to come from the passage that led to the kitchen. It was a loud laugh. The author could only have been Harry Lewis. The laugh was growing louder.

Maria grabbed Apple's arm. "Quick. I cannot take one more repeat of Harry's story about when he directed a school play, in Hollywood, Kansas."

They hurried out.

Within five minutes, having followed directions, Apple was parking the 2CV beside a short-order stand, its vendor wearing soiled whites and a chef's hat. Although this wasn't what Apple had had in mind, he nevertheless nodded gamely when Maria asked, "A hot dog, Arnold?"

They were served one each. Apple drove away singlehanded. The dog was surprisingly good. He wished he had bought another couple. Chewing slowly, he listened to Maria as she went on with the story of her life as an entertainer, which had been prompted by Apple asking if she had found work yet. She interrupted herself only to give directions.

They drove around the bay and into a housing development. It was on a hillside, the road winding up past villas and weed-choked building plots. The snack was finished by the time they parked in a houseless dead-end road.

Ahead lay the town. It was seen merely as a mass of lights, which were doubling themselves in the sea, where they mocked their landbound twins by shimmying suggestively. Between, an ocean liner twinkled as prettily as if it were on a travel poster.

Maria came across the seat, shuffling herself close. She asked, "Is this how you sat in that romantic spot with Mona?"

While Apple was explaining about the unromantic quarry, he idly put his arm along the seat back. He ended, "It was hardly a lovers' lane kind of situation."

"But you must have kissed her. Like this."

Their mouths met. Maria's was warm and swarmy, Apple's submissive due to confusion. He had become two entities. His emotions were erotically aroused, his mind was full of doubt.

All this was too easy, Apple pointed out to himself. And why did she never give a straight answer to questions?—for all her talk, it still wasn't clear if she'd found work. How come she knew about this particular, isolated place?

Apple realized that all along he had tended to discount Maria as a force to be reckoned with, mission-wise, because he had preferred to think of her on another, randier level.

Opening his eyes, which had closed for the kissing, Apple glanced around as far as his position allowed. It wasn't very far. He eased back from the kiss and took a good, circling scan of the area. He saw nothing amiss.

Maria lifted a hand to his neck. "What is it, Arnold?"

"I have to be getting back."

"Nonsense. We have only just arrived here. We have only just started."

His head was pulled down into another meeting of lips, and somehow his left hand found its way inside the front of her dress. There was no barrier of bra.

Maria said, "Mmm."

Apple stretched his fingers to encompass one of the large, vibrant breasts. He was tautly aware of Maria's insinuating tongue and of her hand on his thigh.

Mind said leave at once, body said stay.

Apple fumed at his stupidity for continuing to embrace, kiss, and fondle the girl. He refused to have anything to do with the palm that was slowly rotating over the breast. He was offended by the hand that stroked upward on his leg.

There came the low rumble of a motor. Apple snatched back from the kiss and twisted his head around. A car, with only its parking lights on, had turned into the dead-end road.

Apple freed himself from the embrace swiftly. He said, "Someone's coming."

"Lovers," Maria said. "A couple in search of solitude."

Starting the engine, Apple twisted the wheel viciously and went into a screechy reverse, Maria the while asking what on earth he was playing at. She went on in similar vein, her voice getting harder, as he drove forward and toward the exit. He flicked his headlights up.

There were two men in the other car. They were as good as in disguise, having long hair, or wigs. An anomaly was clothing that looked dark and staid.

"See?" Maria said. "A couple."

Apple didn't argue, nor when next he was told that he was being ridiculous. He was relieved to be passing the other car without incident. He turned out of the dead end.

"Sorry about that," Apple said. "I'd suddenly remembered something I have to do. A cable. I must send one to my grandmother. Her birthday's tomorrow."

Not bad, he thought, which was compensation for the possibility that he might, after all, be seeing this totally wrong—therefore destroying a delicious situation.

Apple changed his mind about that a moment later. A pair of dim lights had come into sight in his rearview mirror. He changed gear and pressed his foot to the floor.

The 2CV, being on a downhill slope, shot forward. Maria was thumped back into her seat. She snapped that he was acting like a maniac, adding, "Nothing can be so urgent."

Apple said absently, "You only have one grandmother."

"Stop at once."

"Can't. Sorry."

"I would rather walk than ride with a madman. I could get killed."

At a maniacal sixty miles an hour, Apple went along one stretch of road and then another. The twin lights stayed behind. They had started to catch up when he covered the final stretch and came out onto the highway. He headed for town.

With Maria muttering peevishly and the car behind drawing even closer, Apple drove full out. Soon he was in a built-up area and getting into traffic. He slowed, but not until he had put several vehicles between himself and the car behind.

He felt safe now. He also felt, again, that he could have been wrong about the whole situation. Tentatively he suggested to his companion that after he had sent the telegram . . .

"No, thank you," Maria said, all frost. "I have suddenly remembered something vital I must do. In fact, you can drop me there. Right there."

They were in a busy spot near the docks, with a heavy sprinkling of pedestrians. Apple steered into the side. As he stopped, the tail car came level, seemed to hesitate, went on.

"You may give me a cigarette," Maria said. "And a light."

During the process, Apple tried to get the atmosphere back to its previous warmth. He was telling himself that the men could have been looking for someone else, among a dozen other possible reasons for their presence.

"Thank you," Maria said, puffing smoke. "And good night." She got out and stalked across the road. Apple sat listlessly watching the smooth cavort of her hips. His eyes reddened with regret.

The back door opened and someone began to get in.

Apple jerked his upper body around. It was a flinch of a movement, more instinctive than rationally directed. His right arm came up in an act of protection.

The intruder spoke, in English. "Cornfield," he said. "Good evening, Six."

Apple steadied, lowering his arm. Cornfield was the code word for this operation, and his number name in it was the one just given. He said, trying for the blasé response, "Good evening, whoever."

"Fourteen," the man said. He settled back on the seat and closed the door. "I think it might rain." He was thirtyish, average in build and features and colouring, wearing a plain suit with a dark tie. He could have passed for almost any nationality and been anything from a waiter to a doctor. He was one of the herd.

"A spot of rain wouldn't hurt," Apple said. "But I don't suppose you came to talk about the weather."

"Actually, Six, I'm not here to talk about anything. Simply to guide you to a certain spot. Shall we go?"

"With pleasure."

"Or we can use my car, if you prefer. These wandering Nissen huts are the end."

"But they work," Apple said. He turned to face the front. "Guide away."

For the third time that day Apple drove out of town. He was pleased by this development but wished Agent Fourteen wouldn't spoil his own image, and tarnish the good entrance he had made, by pettishly pointing out all the 2CV drawbacks. There was nothing worse, Apple thought, than a car snob.

Five miles out of town, by a service station, they turned off the highway onto a decrepit road, which they left after half a mile for a road in even worse condition. It ended against a gate. Fourteen did the opening-and-closing job.

Back inside he said, "Straight across the field."

They bounced over a meadow. Gradually the headlights picked out a cluster of prefabricated buildings. They looked to be returning to their origins—pieces. Apple asked if that was where they were going.

"Sort of," Agent Fourteen said. "Stop around the other side."

What appeared in the headlights when Apple had steered around the buildings was a helicopter. Its blades were droopily still. From inside the cabin of the two-seater aircraft a light gleamed.

"Leave your big lights on, please," Fourteen said. "Come on. You have to board the chopper."

They got out. Apple went ahead, walking toward the helicopter. He changed tack when the agent called, "Other side. You happen to be the pilot."

Cheerfully mystified, Apple went to the far door. He drew it open. The man who sat in the passenger seat said, "Hello, Porter."

Apple hoped, but didn't believe, that he stifled a facial

show of surprise. "Good evening, sir," he said in a businesslike manner. "You want me to take this thing up?"

Angus Watkin nodded. "If you haven't forgotten how. Light aircraft, operation and basic knowledge of, was part of your training, I dare say."

Dare because you know damn well it was, Apple mused as he got in. He fastened his safety belt and bent over the controls. In thirty seconds, he had started the motor and set the blades turning; another thirty, and the helicopter was jerking up off the ground. The noise made Apple grimace.

He nodded with relief, once they were airborne, when his chief lifted a set of earphones with throat mike and gestured to another. Apple put on the set, which reduced the racket to the pounding of a pneumatic drill.

Through the earphones came "Is this thing working, Porter?"

"Yes, sir. We're in contact."

"Excellent. Now circle the field while you make a report on your progress in this mission."

Banking into a turn, Apple said, "Well, sir, I really haven't made any progress. Not yet. I've only been here three days, after all."

"Oddly enough, Porter, I do happen to know how long you've been on the scene. However. Hasn't anything at all been going on?"

"Yes, sir, but nothing that's leading anywhere. At least, not so far as I can see."

"Tell me," Watkin said with one of his little sighs, which lost some of its accusatory character in transit through the intercom. "Give me all the bits and pieces."

Apple talked cautiously, feeling his way. He was hoping that, in the recounting of events, he would see any discrepancy before he actually put its context into words, so could pounce before his chief did.

Apple told of the ledger page, but made no mention of the Yard Card. Watkin would probably interpret its appearance as a statement from the one who had planted it that the Arnold Barker cover was blown, and pull his operative out. To prevent that, to stay in the game, Apple was willing to risk the silence-lie.

Other than that, he told all that had happened as they went on making circles above the field. Frequently Watkin asked questions. He gave no answers, made no comments. When asked, "What could that have meant, sir?" he said, "I'm no wiser than you, Porter." Most of his questions concerned Jason Lock.

Apple said, "He does seem to be pretty suspicious. But then, they all do."

"That, of course, is the problem. The only way to get at the truth is to fish along."

"Has there been any word of George Trent, sir?"

Angus Watkin's blunt negative had an ominous ring, framed as it was in the menace of static. Apple said quickly, "Matter of fact, the scorpion thing was the only definite, obvious thrust in my direction. And even that could've been a prank."

In the tone he always used to convey that he considered himself to be in the company of a fool, Angus Watkin said, "Of course it could."

"I mean, that hit-and-run. I can't see Mrs. Arkwright doing any reckless driving."

"Or loaning her car to someone else, or arranging for it to be stolen, or . . . But I mustn't ramble on. I haven't had my dinner yet. Here's a present for you."

From an inside pocket of his sober suit he produced a gun.

The revolver was small, snub-nosed, and had merely the framework of a butt; a compact and lightweight weapon.

Apple took it gingerly. He was nervous of guns. After putting it to gentle rest inside his shirt he asked about type.

"Point twenty-five," Watkin said. "Not exactly a cannon. But it gives the minimum of trouble with its presence, makes very little noise, has no recoil to speak of, and is accurate so long as the target isn't more than five yards off, in a strong light."

"Thank you, sir. Do I have to sign for it?"

"No, Porter. We British are less diffident about guns than we used to be. It's even nowadays openly admitted that the Queen's personal detective is armed. Whereas for years the subject was politely ignored."

After a moment, knowing Watkin's preference for giving answers rather than straight information, Apple said, "Any further instructions, sir?"

"None whatever. The meeting is over. Take this contraption down, please."

As Apple obeyed, sweeping toward the splash of headlights below, he wondered why there had been a meeting at all. He had learned nothing. All he had been given was the gun, which could have been delivered by a courier, such as Fourteen. But perhaps the fact of the weapon was in itself the message: Beware: Things are hotting up.

That could have been the reason, and not reality, that made Apple think the next morning that there was an air of tension in the house. He sensed it, or seemed to, when he came down to breakfast. But there again, it might have been the odd fact of all the guests sitting at the same table in the dining room.

Although he was greeted politely by Mrs. Arkwright,

Harry Lewis, Jason Lock, and Maria Sola, they didn't invite him to make up a five. Through their talk, as he chose another table, he understood that this camaraderie was an extension of last night's excitement, when they had all pitched in to help at kitchen-crisis time.

Sitting, Apple felt pressure on his stomach. It was the gun. Having no holster, he had been forced to carry the revolver tucked behind his belt, where it was hidden by his wearing a shirt outside his jeans.

Apple was not happy about the weapon, though he accepted the sense of keeping it on him. Trouble was, the gun jiggled about if he walked, and prodded if he sat. Worse, right now it was pointing straight at his groin.

What if the jiggling knocked off the safety catch? What if in sitting the trigger should . . . ?

Apple snapped his mind away from awful possibilities. His voice, however, had a squeakiness as he looked up now to say good morning to Martha, who was putting down his food.

After a moment's chat she left. Apple, under cover of the table, brought his gun out long enough to check the safety. He cleared his throat and started to eat.

The others began to leave—Maria first and without giving the lone diner a glance. Left alone was Harry Lewis. As he too got up from the table, Apple said, "Before you came here to Ibiza, Harry, had you always lived in Philadelphia?"

"Arnold, I certainly had."

"Well now, that's interesting."

"All except for a couple of years as a kid, when I went to high school in Hollywood, Kansas."

So there goes another blunt lead, Apple thought. He switched to asking casual questions about George Trent. The American seemed either bored or worried. He said finally, after a series of dull answers, that he had to go to church. "It's Sunday, y'know."

Apple hadn't known. But following breakfast he found a bucket, a cloth, and went through the back way to the car. He thought a wash was deserved. He had become quite fond of the yellow Citroën. During the job, he left his gun under the seat.

Back in the pension, although there was no one around, the ambience of tension persisted. Apple hoped it wasn't merely on account of a clash of personalities, either guest or staff.

He went up to his room, left the door open, and lay on the bed. So that he wouldn't fall asleep, he used the old Japanese trick of intertwining his fingers and positioning the locked hands upside down on his chest.

When Apple awoke, it was nearly lunchtime. His wrists ached. He had a scanty wash and went downstairs to the dining room, where he was first. He was midway through his meal, served by Martha, before the others began to come in. They took separate tables. There was little talk. Mrs. Arkwright had a book, the American a newspaper, and Maria buffed her fingernails between plying the cutlery.

Jason Lock failed to appear, though Apple waited until he again was the only diner in the room. He had decided that the ex-dentist ought to be talked to at greater length.

Apple went up to Lock's room. Getting no answer to his several taps, he went out to the car and drove to the topless beach. He was there for two hours, strolling about, and whenever he remembered to look for Jason Lock, he looked, but didn't see him.

Apple drove to three other beaches before returning to town. In the Royal Rose, he noted, the atmosphere was unchanged. He went into the bar, where Harry Lewis sat nursing a beer.

"Harry, have you seen Mr. Lock?"

"Arnold, I haven't. What you should do is, you should ask the old girl. She'll know."

Apple found Mrs. Arkwright in the dining room, setting out chessmen on a board. As he walked in she asked, "Have you seen Mr. Lock?"

"Why, no," Apple said. "Were you looking for him?"

"Only for our evening game, Mr. Barker," the Englishwoman said, bending back over the board. "Excuse me."

Apple returned to the bar. While standing at the counter, from where he could keep a watch through the glass doors, he had a desultory conversation with Harry about rugby versus American football. One hour and two sherries on the rocks later, he saw Martha appear across the lobby.

The large girl came over and inside. She wore an expression that was a mixture of concern and the intrigued. "Guess what," she said.

Apple and Harry said, "What?"

"Old Mr. Lock's checked out."

Behind the bar, Harry straightened. "Just like that?"

"Yes. Never said a word to anyone. And he's left a bill."

"No, he hasn't," Mona said, appearing from behind Martha, who asked, "Are you sure?"

"Quite sure." She wore an exaggeration of her standard face of worry.

Apple asked, "He left no note, no forwarding address, nothing?"

Mona: "Nothing. Only an empty, tidy room."

"Who left what?" This question came from Mrs. Arkwright, whom Apple saw standing squatly in the doorway as the other two women moved aside and started to explain in unison.

Throughout, the Englishwoman shook her head. At length she said, "I don't believe it. What rubbish."

Mona spread her hands. "What else can it mean, Alicia?"

"I don't know. We shall have to ponder the situation."

Harry said, "This calls for a drink, folks. On me. Okay?"

The women agreed. Apple declined. He left the bar and went upstairs. He found the ex-dentist's room as described. There was nothing amiss. There were no holes in the ceiling. Apple left and went back down to the lobby.

Passing the bar, where the others had been joined by Maria Sola, he went outside. All the doorways across the street were deserted. Apple moved cautiously along beside the wall. He stopped when right next to the bar window. Though it was closed, he could hear clearly the voices of the five people inside.

Disappointingly, they were discussing alternative motives for Jason Lock's having left—an emergency recall to England, sudden sickness. The talk stayed innocuous until the meeting began to break up. Apple went back the other way.

He circled to the car. For more than an hour he drove around town, taking any way that presented itself. He kept an eye out for Jason Lock while playing with solutions of his own to explain that man's disappearance. He had no success. The only satisfaction he drew from the drive was in realizing that he had grown used to and unworried about the presence of his gun.

Apple entered the pension via the patio, where he was told by the parrot that he was a dope, and where Maria and Harry sat at separate tables. His smile at the Spanish girl going unanswered, Apple took a table himself.

Mrs. Arkwright came stumping in. Her painted face was alive with importance. The ambience that had throbbed with consequence all during the day, it took on a new strength. Martha, carrying a tray, pulled up short on entering.

Thumping her cane on the tiles, Mrs. Arkwright said in ringing tones, "Mr. Lock did not check out of this establishment."

That was followed by silence, during which glances were exchanged, and which lasted until Mona appeared. Her audience now complete, the Englishwoman said, "Mr. Lock's suitcases are up in the attic."

Apple slapped on the brakes. Screeching, the yellow car came to a halt on the suburban street. Apple got out and strode to the hardware store he had just passed. It was still open, though on the verge of closing. He went in and bought a flashlight, which he tried out on the darkness while walking back to the car.

Getting in, he set off driving as swiftly as the Citroën could go and the area allowed. He was annoyed with himself for staying on through dinner—although cut it short he had, by forgoing dessert. What he ought to have done was make some sort of excuse—headache, no appetite—and pretend to go upstairs, but slipping out through the front door.

Not that Apple had a fact to work on. He didn't even have a clue. It was simply that he felt he had to search somewhere, and the place to start was obvious.

During dinner, sporadic conversation had touched only on the subject of Jason Lock. With one exception, Mrs. Arkwright, the consensus was that the suitcases being upstairs was a good sign (the Englishwoman: "So why were they hidden behind others?"). Lock had needed to leave at once because of some emergency and would be coming back. He had told no one for the simple reason that, being siesta time, there was no one around to tell. He would write or telephone.

Maybe, Apple thought now as he turned off onto the dirt road. And maybe not. Only one thing was sure all round: his compatriot didn't know what was going on. Was she the only one in the dark?

Before he reached the point where the track began to climb, Apple turned off onto the unfenced land. He threaded between almond trees, crunching over twigs and leaves left from the recent picking. When he felt himself to be far enough from the dirt road, he stopped and switched off the motor, killed the lights, got out.

Soon on the road again, he headed for the incline. His flashlight he used only intermittently; a quarter-moon gave a fair light and the road's dust stood out greyly from the surrounding summer-end brown.

Apple went at a jog on the climbing, winding track. When one side began to drop away, he moved to the other. He kept one hand on his shifting revolver.

Apple's first feeling as he reached the parking plateau was almost disappointment. He had vaguely thought he would find a black car there. After flashing his light around briefly to make sure, he started up the zigzag paths.

Again dust gleamed a pewter colour to pick out the way. Apple climbed at a sturdy pace. The breeze, strengthening with altitude, moaned around him and played games with his shirt.

Chilled, Apple arrived on the top level. It seemed deserted. He could see the trees silhouetted against the sky, pick out on ground level the deeper darkness of the holes. He began to wander among the inverted, hollowed pyramids.

The hand that touched his shoulder, it became a branch end when Apple, gagging, swung around with the flashlight blazing. He sagged, sweaty on top of his gooseflesh.

Recovered, he went on. He moved in a crouch; if he could see the trees, he had reasoned, his own form would present an equally clear silhouette to someone else.

If anyone else around here there was, Apple mused, knowing he was trying to talk himself into leaving without going any further. The place was as antipathetic to him as on his first visit; worse than; then, he'd had company.

Over the moan of the breeze came another sound. Apple stopped to listen. He thought it could be a car. But he had made that same mistake before.

Sound fading, Apple made to go on. His body swayed forward, then back, pushed by the fact of his having seen a patch of paleness. It was in the pit immediately to his left.

Sinking to one knee, Apple shone the flash. What it picked out was an arm. Sweat again came to cover his chilled skin as Apple stared down at what appeared to be a disembodied limb. Next, he saw that the rest of the figure could be, must be, hidden behind the adjacent huddle of broken sandstone blocks.

Heart tapping, Apple began to go down the smooth, sloping side of the pit. Its smell of refuse and stagnant water took strength as he went lower. Near the bottom he circled, halted, and aimed his flash.

The white arm belonged to the white suit of Jason Lock. He was lying spread-eagled on his back. As neat as always, he would have looked to be peacefully asleep except for the blood on his forehead.

From beyond the pit came a noise. Apple snapped off the light in the manner taught in Training Five: he slammed the face of the flash against his shirt.

The noise came again. It sounded like a human voice. Putting off the flashlight properly, Apple began to scramble up the slope. At once he slipped and slid back. He bent down to one hand and set off like a three-legged animal. He reached the top.

Cautiously he raised his head above the rim. Toward the exit pathways he could see two individual splashes of light. They were beaming from side to side. They were coming this way.

Apple quickly crab-walked up onto the level and then down into another pit, and then up again and over the top like cannon fodder. In the next hole he felt safer. He risked a peek above the level.

The flashlights had moved farther away from one another. They were still approaching. Behind them there was nothing to be seen of the carriers, though Apple could hear the gentle thud of their footsteps in the ground near his head.

A beam suddenly swept toward him. He ducked; in time, he hoped. He went further down into the pit. Lying still, he put a hand inside his shirt and onto the butt of the gun.

The thuds went on, growing louder. After a minute they became fast, jumbled and erratic, like the sound of falling logs. Apple understood this to mean that the torchbearers had found the ex-dentist.

After a pause, the thuds restarted. Now they were ponderous, spaced, and on the wane. Apple crept up the slope. With less caution he peered over the rim.

It was an odd sight. Jason Lock, gleaming brightly and whitely, seemed to be floating away over the ground, feet first. Some seconds passed before Apple realized that the Englishman was being carried by the two people, who, slickly, held the torches in their mouths. The rear light shone down on Jason Lock.

Quietly, Apple got out of the pit. Not until the trio ahead were beginning to dim in darkness did he go forward. He stayed in a crouch and kept to the same pace even when the others had sunk from sight on the downward paths.

Arriving at that point himself, Apple knelt to watch. The mysterious pair zagged down to the plateau, where the leader's light picked out a medium-size grey car. Into its back was hustled the limp form of Jason Lock, into its front got the pair. Motor and headlights came alive. By the backwash of the latter, Apple saw clearly the two people in front. They were Hippie and Maria Sola. The car drove off.

Apple ran. With the grey car gone from sight, he was able to use his flash constantly. Its beam wavered about the downward path as he ran; rather, as he declined to put a brake on his gravity-towed rush. At any moment he expected to stumble and go flying head over toes.

With a final jump that jolted every inch of his body, Apple landed on the parking plateau. He ran to its exit track. Though the car wasn't to be seen below, a glow from the headlights showed location. Apple was appreciative now of the narrow and dangerous road. It needed to be taken at a careful speed.

Himself, he took no precautions as he ran on down the hill, save to keep well away from that sheer drop. He used his flash except when the grey car came briefly into view on bends.

Apple thought that there was a good chance of his reaching the Citroën in time to give chase. Apart from that, he didn't think into the situation.

The gun slipped. Apple caught his breath and started on an untidy halt. His slap to the waist was too late: the revolver had gone down inside his jeans.

Once stopped, he put down the flash to fumble with his belt. He had that unbuckled and was shooting down the zip when he realized that the gun had slid down into the jeans' left leg.

Nevertheless he opened up. Delving past the permanent obstacles, his fingertips scrabbled on the revolver. It sank further. He groaned in exasperation, and, sticking his leg out, began to shake it. The gun descended slowly.

While leg-shaking, Apple looked around. The headlights were still there, but faint, far off. Any minute now the car would be hitting level, and would then be able to speed up.

A last, large kick brought the gun free. Lunging a stoop, Apple grabbed it quickly. He fumbled belt and zip into place, picked up the flash, ran on.

By shortcutting across land between hairpin bends he saved a lot of yardage. He reached the flat and set off over fields, crow-flying toward the Citroën. His breathing was laboured. In the distance, the headlights were growing faint by the second.

Apple came to his car. He slammed inside, tossed gun and flash onto the other seat, started the motor, and leapt away. He silently thanked the 2CV's makers for its ground clearance and elastic suspension as he went bounding across the rough land.

It was the same on the track, with its holes and lumps. There was no need to drive with care. All Apple had to do was keep his head down so that it didn't get slammed on the roof as the car bounced and cavorted.

The lights ahead grew stronger.

Soon, Apple was able to slow down; he wanted to stay out of sight. He drove with only his side lights on, which he could just about do, thanks to the quarter-moon. The revolver he put back behind his belt.

The grey car reached the highway and put on speed. Apple kept well back. He even allowed other vehicles to take positions in the gap between. He would not, he knew, lose the other car.

Suburbs graded into dreary being. They had still to become citified when the grey car turned right. Apple took the same corner, slowing because there was now no traffic between to hide behind.

After two blocks on the ill-lit street, he reduced to a crawl: the other car had swung onto a forecourt. It was in front of a clinic. Steps led up to a doorway which was topped with the sign EMERGENCY.

The grey car stopped. Moving swiftly, Hippie and Maria got out, opened the rear door, and drew Jason Lock outside. They carried him to the steps, put him down gently, and ran back to the car. It shot away with a screech of rubber. The whole operation had taken less than half a minute.

Apple drove on in cautious pursuit. As he drew level with the clinic, an intern was coming out, his incurious gaze on the man whose clothes were soap-ad whiter than his own. The impression he gave was of all this being routine.

After its burst of racing to leave the clinic, the grey car had settled to a steady, normal pace. It was headed away from the town centre. Apple had no trouble keeping it in sight, even though he stayed far back, the reason for both being that there was scant traffic on these quiet residential streets.

He felt relaxed enough to get out a cigarette and light up, though he flared his lighter only when the lead car had turned a bend.

Apple was squashing out the butt in the ashtray when the stoplights on the grey car flashed. Suburbs left behind now, there were the walls of private estates on either hand. Near a gateway in one of these the lead car halted.

Apple got lucky. A service lane appeared on his right. Otherwise, he would have had to choose between stopping on the road, which would be suspicious, or driving past Hippie and Maria, who would see him.

Apple steered into the lane, stopped, and got out. He went back to the road. Maria was walking from the car to the gates. She opened them and went through. The car followed. The gates closed.

Apple ran. On reaching the gateway, it was to see the car's taillights flicking through trees. Beyond that, several glowing windows showed where a house stood.

Apple tried the gates. They were locked. He went along beside the wall, looking at it appraisingly. It was about eight feet high but drystone, built of uncemented rocks. There were ample hand- and toeholds. And being tall would be a help.

Apple debated going back to get the flashlight. Deciding not, impatient, he chose a spot and began to climb. He was quickly astride the top. He felt like sitting on there for a moment, but a car was approaching on the highway.

Letting himself down to an arm's-length grip, that left a drop of only a few inches. On the ground he turned. The car didn't show up in the darkness ahead, either by shape or by lights. In the house, another window was glowing.

The dog. Apple twitched strongly on seeing it. He had been about to move forward when, shortening his gaze to the underfoot ahead, he had seen the dog there, four or five feet away, directly in his path.

The animal stood out palely in the moonlight. Its colouring would be something like his own, Apple mused to help him settle from the shock. That and the size made him recognize the dog for a Podenco Ibizenco, a breed peculiar to the island. It was similar to a greyhound but with longer legs and a rougher coat.

The physical detail that interested Apple most at the moment was the teeth. They were gleamingly on show. This seemed to be more ominous because of the fact that the dog was silent. It was also still. There was no movement anywhere, from the end of the tail to the tip of the long head.

Dismissing the absurd hope that he was looking at a statue, Apple moved his right foot forward. He stopped immediately on hearing a low growling. It continued until he had drawn his foot back.

So that was that, Apple thought. He wasn't about to try to best a guard dog for the privilege of getting close to the house. And what could he do if he did get there? Knock and ask for a glass of water?

Apple didn't care for his defeatism, until he reminded himself that all this could have nothing whatever to do with Arnold Barker, with drugs, with the KGB, with George Trent. It could be an entirely personal matter.

Taking a step backwards, unaccompanied by growling, Apple mused that he would, of course, return here, though prepared to deal with the Podenco Ibizenco. He'd had enough for one day. He was exhausted. And, as he had been taught, one of your greatest enemies was tiredness, body working on brain.

Apple turned to the wall. With many wary glances over his shoulder, he climbed, straddled the top, and let himself down on the other side. He set off back to his car. It had never even occurred to him that he could have shot the dog.

CHAPTER 4

As the knocking grew louder, Maria's naked body began to dissolve. He tried to hold it back, ignore the intruding noise. But the knocks went on. They had the persistence of brutality. Maria dwindled away into nothing and he came reluctantly to the surface of consciousness.

Apple rolled over in bed. The knocks were coming from the door. He slewed a look at his watch and saw that it was ten o'clock. Gruffly he called out, "Just a minute."

A female voice, rendered void of identity by the wood, asked, "You're awake now?"

"Yes. Just about."

"And decent?"

"Yes, I am," Apple said. "And if you'll give me a minute to—"

There was a click, and the door opened. "Master key," Mrs. Arkwright said, coming in behind her walking stick. In the other hand she carried a steaming cup. "You're too late for breakfast, so you will have to make do with a coffee."

In a series of fast movements, Apple sat up, scuffled the bedding neat, patted his hair, held a sheet up to his chest. He said, "Yes. Thank you."

Pointedly leaving the door open, which Apple found appealing, Mrs. Arkwright handed over the cup and saucer. "When you're ready, Mr. Barker, we'd like you to join us downstairs."

"Us, ma'am?" Apple asked, then regretted at once having used *ma'am*. It made the Englishwoman's propriety with the door seem foolish.

"Mona, Martha, Mr. Lewis, Miss Sola, myself. All of us. We have been waiting for you. We are having, in fine, a council of war."

"About what?" He sipped coffee. "Jason Lock?"

"Precisely," Mrs. Arkwright said, her painted face aggressive. "Some of us are convinced that there has been foul play or an accident. Others are not so sure. We need a deciding vote. You understand?"

"Not quite."

"We have to decide whether or not to take action."

"Good. But what kind of action?"

"That will have to be discussed," Mrs. Arkwright said, turning to the door. "Please do not keep us waiting long, Mr. Barker."

Alone, Apple finished his coffee, got up, and went along to the bathroom. He didn't know how he was going to play the coming scene. He didn't even know if Jason Lock was dead or merely injured. All he did know for sure was that he wanted to get away as quickly as possible in order to investigate the mystery villa.

Fifteen minutes later, Apple walked into the bar. Harry, standing behind the counter like a judge, said, "Now let's have a bit of order, ladies."

That was the signal for everyone to start talking at once. Apple listened to the jabber, turning from face to face. He included the American, who himself had joined in the talk.

Slowly, Apple gathered that the foul-play/accident theory was held by Martha and Mrs. Arkwright. Harry Lewis and Maria were sure that Lock would be coming back hale and hearty, perhaps any minute now. Mona, while looking more concerned than usual, took the position that no news was good news.

The talk began to run down. Everybody looked at Apple expectantly. He chose the Spanish girl, asking, "So what do you think could be behind this sudden departure—if it's in all innocence?"

Maria said, "We have been through that, Arnold. There are many possibilities. He is a big boy and able to take care of himself."

Mrs. Arkwright thumped the floor with her stick. "That could also have been said of George Trent."

"But who was this Trent, please?"

Talk rose again. Apple couldn't help admire Maria. Her face was the picture of innocence. No one would have guessed that a few hours ago she had been helping to carry the missing man.

Martha got up and clapped her hands. Into the following silence she said, "Who cares about George Trent? That's ancient history. It's Mr. Lock we've got to think about. He was a nice old boy, and something's got to be done."

Harry Lewis shook his head. "Martha, that guy could be on his way here this morning. He'd be kind of angry, seems to me, if he found that a fuss was being made."

"But we can't just *sit* here."

Mona said, "Harry's right, Martha. You know what a quiet, retiring person Jason is. He'd be mortified. Maybe offended. He might even check out of here altogether. That I can do without."

Martha looked at her stonily. "That's a very selfish attitude."

After wincing, Mona lifted her chin. "I'd rather you didn't talk to me like that, if you don't mind."

Martha opened her mouth, closed it again, turned

abruptly, and stalked out of the bar. Her heavy footfalls echoed around the lobby.

Mrs. Arkwright said, "Even though she's not here, her vote still counts. That's two for, two against, one abstention."

"The abstainer's me," Mona told Apple. "Do you think I am being selfish?"

"I think you're being sensible."

She smiled. "Thank you. Does that mean that you're one of the againsts?"

Apple scratched his head. "I don't know. But it seems to me that this is the kind of thing that happens constantly in hotels and boarding houses."

In a loud aside to no one in particular, Mrs. Arkwright said, "The man's an idiot."

"Arnold, you are so right," Harry said. "It's accepted as part of the business, an occupational hazard, like supermarkets allowing for a certain amount of shoplifting."

Mrs. Arkwright created a hiss by drawing in a long, long breath through her nose, the while glaring at the man behind the bar. There was still a hiss-like quality in her voice when she at last spoke.

"Are you suggesting, sir, that Mr. Lock has left because of some sordid financial reason?"

While Harry was fumbling for words, Apple offered, "I'm sure Mr. Lock is too nice a person to do anything underhand."

Mrs. Arkwright, aside: "Intelligent lad."

"Yes," Maria said. "But what do *you* think he could have done with himself, Arnold?"

Apple was taken by the strong temptation to edge close to the truth, or as much of it as he knew. He wanted to see how Maria would react. He thought he might learn something therefrom.

Resisting, he said, "Well, it's just occurred to me that he

could have gone off for a tour of the island. By car." He turned toward the Englishwoman. "Maybe he borrowed yours, Mrs. Arkwright."

"That would be terribly clever of him," she said grittily. "I do not possess a motorcar."

"Oh? I must have been mistaken. I thought I saw you driving a black Seat the other day."

"That, Mr. Barker, is a machine which belongs to Martha."

"Is someone taking my name in vain?" asked the New Zealander, striding into the bar. "Good-o." She had a satisfied expression.

Apple explained. Martha said offhandedly, "Some chap I met left it with me while he took a trip."

Harry accused, "You're looking real pleased with yourself."

"For a good reason," Martha said. "See, I decided to cast the final vote myself."

Maria shook her head. "That is impossible."

"Who cares? I cast it and I did something positive."

"What?"

"I telephoned the police. They're on their way here now. No one has to leave."

Domingo Sanchez of the Civil Guard was young to be a captain. No more than thirty, he had a smooth pink face that looked as if it had never felt a razor. His eyes were soulful, his lips thin and firm. He held his short slim body ramrod stiff, as if as a warning: Don't think I'm young and soft.

Older was the other uniformed man. He had nothing to say, and had nothing to do except keep in the background, look severe, and hold his superior's patent-leather headgear. His presence, Apple knew, was because Civil Guards never worked singly.

Everyone was in the dining room. Some unspoken, mutual

agreement born of instinct had taken the pension people there, into respectability, away from the irreputable atmosphere of a bar.

The six people stood or sat in a rough semicircle facing the captain, who was standing. He had just returned from a half-hour examination of the missing man's room and effects. Those thirty minutes had put a severe strain on Apple's patience. He was aching to get back to the walled villa.

Captain Sanchez looked up from his notebook. In excellent English he said, "From your preliminary statements, ladies and gentlemen, it appears that there is a little disagreement over the hour of Mr. Lock's disappearance."

Mona began to explain, for the second time, that everyone was guessing, for no one could be sure about a thing like that. Domingo Sanchez listened politely, his head inclined, his eyes on the crossed legs of Maria Sola.

Apple longed to say: Why don't you telephone the hospitals? But Arnold Barker, who worked with animals, wouldn't know about such automatic procedures.

The captain straightened his head to its West Point erectness. "Thank you, Mrs. Smith," he said. "So it is impossible to say who was the last person to see Mr. Lock?"

"I believe I was," Mrs. Arkwright said, raising a forefinger. "That would have been at about four o'clock."

"Was his comportment in any way unusual?"

"Yes, it was. That's why I feel sure something's wrong. Mr. Lock was agitated. Which is out of character."

"Did you and he have converse, Mrs. Arkwright?"

"Briefly, yes. He said he had somewhere to go. I told him not to forget our game—chess, you know—and he simply smiled. That was all."

The captain said, "Which, with the agitation, could of

course fit with a person who was on the point of slipping away covertly."

"Course it could," Harry Lewis blustered. He was standing beside Maria's chair. "And what's more, I'm pretty sure I saw Jason later than that. About five o'clock, as I've already said."

"And was he agitated, Mr. Lewis?"

"Captain, he was not. I was in the bar and saw him crossing the lobby. He looked fine to me. Just fine. That was at five."

Mrs. Arkwright told the floor that people who spent half their lives behind bars rarely knew what time it was.

"Behind bars?" Domingo Sanchez asked, looking at Harry. "You have been in prison, Mr. Lewis?"

As the American started to sort that out, wearing a forced manner of amusement, Apple made to pat his stomach to soothe its nervous quirkings. At once he felt the gun under his shirt. He froze.

Harry said, "See? Just an expression."

"You have no criminal record?"

"Captain, I haven't. None at all."

Mrs. Arkwright hummed a snatch of song while Apple told himself that everyone might get searched and the captain said, "I would like your place and date of birth, Mr. Lewis, please."

Apple weighed the risks. He decided to get rid of the gun. Since making an excuse to leave the room would be too suspicious, it would have to be done here. If it could. If no one paid any attention.

Laughing like a doctor, Harry was giving personal details to the policeman, who wrote busily in his notebook. Mrs. Arkwright was staring at the American with narrowed eyes. On Apple's right, Maria was breathing on a thumbnail; on his left, Martha and Mona were playing strangers at a bus stop.

Apple reached under his shirt. He gripped the gun and brought it up out of his waistband. Eyes constantly roaming and hoping not to meet other eyes, he slowly slid the gun around his body, still underneath the shirt.

"I don't care what anyone thinks," Mrs. Arkwright said. "Mr. Lock and I were close. He would have told me if he were leaving."

Mona said, "I agree with you."

Apple had the revolver at his spine. He took a careful step backwards, thus reaching a table. He sat on its edge and put the gun down onto the cloth. The next step would be to get it out of sight among the centre collection of condiment jars and seasoning bottles.

Closing his notebook, the captain turned to the last speaker. "He left a bill, Mrs. Smith?"

Mona shook her head. "A mere trifle. Nothing."

Martha said, "Yes, but he was the kind of person who would see to trifles."

"Yes indeed," Mrs. Arkwright said. She glared at Harry when he offered, "So that means he must be coming back."

Apple was about to start feeling the gun toward the centre. He stopped on seeing that Domingo Sanchez was looking at him; stopped and brought his hand around to the front. He gave a friendly smile and folded his arms.

The captain said, "Possibly you would like to offer an opinion, Mr. Barker."

"Um—an opinion?"

"On what happened with Mr. Lock."

"I really can't say, Officer. I've been here only a few days. I hardly know the man. Sorry, but I can't help you."

Martha burst out, "Oh yes you can."

Apple winced. "What?"

"Your experience could be a great help, Arnie. I'm sure the captain would be happy to know the truth about you."

As Apple slowly opened his mouth, Domingo Sanchez asked in a hard voice, "What is this, please?"

Martha turned to him. "Mr. Barker is a detective. He's from Scotland Yard. He's got a card to prove it." She tugged Apple's sleeve. "Show him."

Apple waved his hands. "No no, it's a mistake. A joke. I don't know anything about Scotland Yard."

"But you have an identity card," Martha said. "I've seen it. Why are you avoiding the issue? You can help find poor Mr. Lock."

"Listen. That card doesn't mean anything. You can buy them in any London joke shop. They sell thousands to tourists. They take your picture and put it on while you wait."

The captain asked sternly, "Where is this card, Mr. Barker?"

Apple quickly decided against the idea that had occurred to him: saying he had lost the card or thrown it away. Showing it with gusto would work better, be an allayer.

Laughing in a way that reminded him of Harry Lewis a minute ago, Apple brought the piece of cardboard from his hip pocket. "I'm actually quite proud of this. It looks so *real*. I've had great fun with it. What I do is, I leave it lying around to see how the finder reacts. That's how this young lady came to see it. Right?"

Looking disappointed, Martha nodded. Domingo Sanchez's expression was the reverse of disappointment. He said an unfinished "Masquerading as an officer of the law . . ."

"No no, Captain, it's nothing like that."

"Give me the card, please."

"Of course," Apple said. "With pleasure. I know you'll appreciate its near-perfection." He pushed up from his seat on the table, at which point he remembered the gun lying there. It had been driven out of his mind by the Scotland Yard surprise.

He said, "Ah."

Captain Sanchez: "I beg your pardon?"

"Nothing. Nothing."

The policeman held out his hand. "That identity card, if you please."

"Certainly," Apple said, not moving. "Of course." He held the card out, hoping that the captain would come and get it. Sanchez stayed put. Next Apple held the card vaguely in Martha's direction, hoping she might do the delivery. She seemed to have lost interest.

"Mr. Barker," the captain said, his tone lethally gentle. "Be so good as to bring me that card at once."

Apple sighed. He took one step forward. No one said anything, no one gasped, no one pointed. He took another step. Still nothing, except that the policeman was looking at him strangely.

Apple couldn't resist a glance back. The glance became a stare when he saw that the table was empty. The gun had gone. He swung back with a smile, saying, "Yes, the card."

Domingo Sanchez had no smile. He said, "I think you had better come to the police station, Mr. Barker."

It was a large, gaunt room. The walls were ripply with two hundred years of whitewash. From opposite sides, the King and Franco stared at each other coolly. The tiled floor was never silent, though the creators of the squeak and clatter were themselves mostly quiet as they came and went, came and went.

Apple, doubled up on one of the small chairs, smothered another yawn. He was nervous, not tired; frustrated, not bored. This was wasting precious time. This, furthermore, was anticlimax, which played havoc with Apple's sense of theatre. He would have felt better about the whole thing if he had been put in a cell.

Two hours ago Domingo Sanchez had said, "Wait here, please. I shall get busy with the telex." Ten minutes, Apple had thought, for them to find out he wasn't employed by Scotland Yard. What then? Would they accept the joke-shop story?

Apple no longer cared. He wouldn't have minded if they had come in with a thumbscrew. Anything was better than a dead wait.

Swallowing a belch, which seemed to ease his hunger, Apple went back to the intriguing question of who had taken his gun. Two people had been within easy reach of the table: Maria and Martha. But those last couple of minutes, he thought, had been confusing. He hadn't been closely aware of what was going on around him. Only Mona, standing near the captain, was entirely in the clear.

The floor yammered with the stride of authority. Apple looked around, then got to his feet as he saw Domingo Sanchez approaching, his face as neatly arranged as his uniform. He was giving nothing away.

Stopping at a reasonable distance, where he wouldn't have to tilt back his head to look at Apple, the captain said, "Excuse me for taking so long."

Apple hoped that was a good sign. "Perfectly all right."

"You do not, of course, have a criminal record."

"No, of course I haven't."

"Nor, it seems, does Mr. Lewis. He, at least, is quite genuine."

"Well, there you are," Apple said. He smiled. "But you had to check."

Domingo Sanchez nodded. "And while we were engaged

on doing so, another department found the missing gentleman."

"Good. I'm delighted. Was he in a different hotel?"

"No, he is in the Sacred Heart Clinic. With a head wound. It would appear that he fell in a sandstone pit. It is a common accident here for the tourists."

"Is it really? How curious."

"If it was, in fact, an accident," Captain Sanchez said, his face still bland.

Apple frowned. "I'm not sure I understand you, Officer. Is Mr. Lock claiming to have been attacked?"

"Mr. Lock is unable to claim anything at the moment. He is not conscious. He was identified by the papers in his pocket. All that he has mumbled is *quarry*. Which fitted with certain signs on the clothing."

"Is he seriously hurt?"

"As of an hour ago he was," the captain said. "Perhaps he will improve, and when he grows conscious will tell us that he fell in the pit."

"Yes, I'm sure he will."

"And explain the singular matter of the packed suitcases."

"Well, yes."

"And tell us what kind of magic he used to get himself, unconscious, from a sandstone quarry to the clinic."

"Mmm."

The captain came closer. Looking semi-up he said, "But perhaps you are in a position to answer those questions yourself."

Apple blinked. "I, Officer?"

Now emotion did show in the youthful face. What it expressed was disdain. The voice was full of it for an enigmatic "It *is* possible for you to be on holiday, one imagines."

"I should—um—hope so."

With coordinated movements, Captain Sanchez stepped away again and held out the identity card. "This is yours."

"Thanks," Apple said. "Aren't they fun? It's the big gimmick of the season. Last year it was a mocked-up photo of yourself shaking hands with the Prime Minister."

Sanchez allowed his face to show boredom, for the effect. He said, "The card, as you very well know, is genuine. You have been cleared by Scotland Yard. Good day, Detective Inspector Barker."

One minute later Apple was out in the sun-bright street. He put aside the question of the Yard Card for the moment. There was a decision he had to make. Should he now go to the walled villa or to see Jason Lock?

The former was the more tempting, but the latter might be more useful; the former would be there tomorrow, tonight, an hour from now, but the latter could . . .

Not taking the macabre thought any further, even though last night he had believed Lock to be dead, Apple began to look around for a vacant taxi. One soon came along. He got in and said, "Sacred Heart Clinic, please."

It wasn't until they were drawing onto the forecourt that Apple realized he had spoken in English, and been understood. He thought it was a good job he wasn't paranoid. While paying, he made a point of not looking at the driver.

Inside, after the dowdy old streets, the clinic was like something out of the space age. It was all chrome, plastic, and white uniforms. There was the cheery, optimistic atmosphere of an undertaker's on New Year's Eve.

At a glassed-in cubbyhole Apple found a nurse who spoke French but no English. He decided that Arnold Barker would have retained a certain amount of schoolboy French. Using the worst accent he could muster, which for him was as difficult as a skilled musician playing off-key, he asked if he could see the casualty, Jason Lock.

The girl said she would have to get hold of the doctor who was in charge of that particular case. "If you would care to wait in the bar, sir?"

Apple was relieved that, modern though the clinic might be, it hadn't discarded the civilized Spanish custom of having a bar in all places of healing, public or private.

Apple didn't feel like a drink. It was only to be flying in the dried-up face of Anglo-Saxon convention that he ordered a sherry on the rocks. He drank it in the same spirit. The alcohol landed badly on his empty stomach. He ordered a bottle of water.

That was long finished before the nurse came in. The patient, she reported, was out of danger. He was in a normal sleep and couldn't be seen until tomorrow noon at the earliest.

Apple asked, "Did he become conscious?"

"Yes, for a short time, not very long ago."

"He talked?"

"Yes, but the policeman who was waiting couldn't understand English, nor could anyone else who was there."

Leaving, Apple told himself that he had been right in the first place: he ought to have gone to the villa. But, since he had to pass near the pension anyway, to get his car, he might as well go in and prepare to deal with the villa guard dog in a professional manner.

Apple strode away from the clinic. His step seemed peculiarly light. He wondered if he could be feeling the sherry's effects.

The patio was empty, except for the parrot, which said nothing. Also deserted was the lobby, and there was no one to be seen through the glass doors leading to bar and dining room. There was, overall, a curious atmosphere of desertion in the building.

Apple shrugged one shoulder and went swiftly upstairs. He unlocked his door. The grind of the turning key was loud in the silence. Apple stood back to push the door open. But the room was empty. He went in and saw the gun.

It was lying in the middle of the bed, which had been neatly made. After staring at his revolver for a moment, Apple went across and picked it up. It was still loaded. Nor had it been tampered with in any way, Apple found on checking it over, including a probe with a pencil to make sure the barrel hadn't been blocked—which would make the weapon explode in the user's hand when he pulled the trigger.

Apple put the gun behind his belt. Its disappearance and return he would consider later, along with the Yard Card affair. Now he had to think dog.

Folding a towel longwise, Apple wrapped it tightly around his forearm. A safety pin would have been useful, but, not having one, he made do by rolling down his sleeve and buttoning the cuff. That would keep the towel in place.

Apple remembered the routine from Training Two. You allowed or encouraged the dog to clamp its jaws on your wrist. You then grabbed it high on the scruff of the neck and forced the head forward, which kept the jaws firmly and safely in place. After that there were several ways of killing, maiming, or knocking out the animal. Apple intended putting it over to the other side of the wall.

With his left sleeve rolled matchingly down, Apple left the room. There was still silence everywhere. The others, he supposed, would be having siestas. Meaning that the kitchen would be vacant, should a hungry man want to sneak a bite to eat.

In the lobby, Apple was assuring himself that, as a paying

guest, one who had missed a paid-for lunch, he had every right to take a little food, when the entrance door suddenly burst open.

In swarmed the others. Harry Lewis led the way from Mona, Mrs. Arkwright, Martha, and Maria. Faces alive, they came crowding toward Apple, who took an instinctive step backwards.

In unison, the Englishwoman and Martha said, "He's been found."

Also together, Mona and Maria Sola said, "The police let you go, Arnold."

Harry said, "He's in a clinic with a battered head."

Apple, who had nodded at everything, went on nodding while being told how Captain Sanchez telephoned with the news of Jason Lock, how they had all gone to see him in the car that Martha was looking after, and how satisfied the doctor was with his condition.

Mrs. Arkwright said, "I was right, you see, Mr. Barker."

Harry asked, "Arnold, what happened with you and the cops?"

"They checked with London and found out I'd been telling the truth about that joke Scotland Yard card."

"I feel such a fool," Martha said, putting both hands to her face as if she was going to lift it off.

Mona said it was all water under the bridge. "And now we're going to have a bottle of champagne—on the house."

Everybody cheered and moved away. Not knowing how he could get out of the invitation gracefully, Apple followed. He told himself he would stay no longer than ten minutes.

Eleven minutes later, as Harry was opening the second bottle, which he insisted on paying for, Apple said to no one in particular, "Oh well." His appetite had gone. He felt fine.

They were at the bar, all standing except Mrs. Arkwright, who was perched dangerously on a stool. She and Martha were telling each other how very right they had been. Maria was talking over Mona's head to Apple about show business.

Harry replenished the glasses. He asked, grinning, "Did the cops say anything about me?"

Apple nodded. It was easy to nod. His neck seemed rubbery. He said, "Harry, they did. Please believe me that they did."

The grin shortened at one side while at the other it grew longer. "What they say?"

"Tell you later. In confidence." He was unable to gauge the reaction to this, for Harry moved back down the bar to his drink. Apple didn't care. He tuned in again to Maria's views of the entertainment world.

After a minute, finding the monologue tedious, Apple said, "Why don't you hand out a free sample of your work? Sing us a song, Maria?"

The Spanish girl appeared to be dubious. Mona said, "Yes, please do." Martha said, "I'm sure you're great." Mrs. Arkwright said her glass was empty.

Maria performed two songs, the while looking uncomfortable, as if the lyrics were obscene. Her voice, Apple thought, was terrible. Embarrassed by that, he applauded lustily, stopping only when Mona told him that enough was enough.

"No, we haven't," Harry Lewis said. "Folks, we just gotta have another bottle."

Apple made an expansive gesture. "This one's on me."

Mrs. Arkwright said, "And we shall drink a toast to Mr. Lock."

They drank two toasts, the second for every injured person

in the world. Apple told one of his favourite one-liners, about the man who was at death's door and the doctors were trying to pull him through. He was the only one who laughed.

Mona asked, "Were the police decent to you, Arnold?"

Sipping champagne, Apple told a story of being given the third degree, of threats and strong lights and cigar smoke in the face. He coughed, feeling marvellous.

Mona told him he was brave. Mrs. Arkwright said it was time she went to water her geraniums, after which she would have a siesta. She left following a help down from her stool by Martha and Maria, who then began to talk about the roller-disco.

Listening with slow nods, Apple learned that a certain German woman was always causing trouble by thinking that every man was after her. She had several male friends as protectors. Apple smiled shrewdly. He thought it clever of him to have solved that little puzzle. He was red-hot today.

To Mona he said, "Let me tell you what happened at the police station."

"You already did."

If he was repeating himself, Apple mused, it must be because he was slightly, ever so very slightly, drunk. That's what it must be because. It would be better if he went on his way.

"On my way," he said, raising his glass. He drained it and put it down, whereupon it was immediately filled by Harry. Apple would have protested except for having to answer Martha's "Is that a bandage on your wrist, Arnold?"

He said evenly that he had understated the treatment he had been given at the police station. "But I would rather not go into details."

"We'll drink to your survival. Another bottle, Harry. On me."

"That's the spirit," Apple said. He hadn't felt better in his life. He was even growing fond of his rubbery neck.

After that, things became strange and hazy. He seemed mostly to be leaning on someone. At one stage, he found there were soft, female arms around his neck; at another, a gentle voice was saying it would help him to drink. Only one exchange stood out clearly:

A voice asked, "Are you awake?"

He said, "Of course I am."

"Then why don't you open your eyes?"

"They are open. I think."

He was walking—with help. Or perhaps he was helping someone to walk. Either way, he was moving, and then climbing, but with frequent halts while he laughed. He wished he knew what was so funny.

"Just a little further," the voice said. "Not far now."

"I enjoy a good joke," he said. "I really do."

"There'll be more when you wake up from your little nap."

"Li'l nap. Yes. Tell you what, I'll have a li'l nap."

The haziness faded, leaving darkness.

First there was pain. It churned away in the side of his head, seared his right leg, bored into the small of his back. Groaning, obviously, was no help, for he next became aware of the groans and knew that they must be coming from himself.

Third was the taste. His mouth felt as if it had been used as a combination ashtray and garbage disposal. He was still drearily considering that, and trying to rouse saliva from among the dryness, when his sense of smell took a turn.

It was a campfire. But somebody must have thrown rubbish on the flames because the aroma of the smoke lacked charm. It was acrid, stinky, offensive. He hoped there would be a change in the wind.

The stench went on, along with the pain, the groans, and the fetid taste, but another of his senses helped by providing a distraction. Hearing presented him with the sound of bells, the yip-yip of sirens, and a grumbling like that from a restless audience.

Curious, Apple thought, after which he came fully to the surface of consciousness.

He was lying on a floor. By changing position, he ended the pain in his awkwardly placed leg; by rolling over, he escaped the pain being caused by the object underneath him; by sitting up, he made the pain in his head worse.

Giving up anyway on the useless groans, Apple looked around through slitted eyes. It took him several seconds to recognize the place as the storeroom at the top of the house, where he had left the scorpion.

That recollection sent him scrambling to his feet. He stood swaying and holding his head. He saw that the object he had been lying on was his gun. Gently he stooped to get the weapon, which he put back behind his belt.

Apple allowed himself one more groan. It was born not of pain but embarrassment. He realized that he had been disgustingly drunk and had been brought here to sleep it off. He supposed he had made an idiot of himself.

To escape trying to remember every asinine thing he had most likely said and done, Apple went to the window, which showed the beginnings of dusk. He looked out and down.

There was a crowd of people; standing, not passing. Every eye was aimed at either the Royal Rose or one of the three fire engines that were parked at angles on the roadway.

Apple's mind snapped to comparative sharpness. The scene

below, the smell inside, they told him what was going on. The pension was on fire and he was in it.

Apple leapt to the door. There was no movement to his touch. The door had been locked on the other side. But it was old and frail. A few kicks ought to do the trick.

The first kick sent Apple staggering backwards. He tripped and fell over a suitcase. That, when his head pain subsided, made him think of a trunk. He grabbed one after getting up and ran at the door with it. The trunk broke into two halves. It had, however, smashed one upper panel in the door.

Apple wriggled his arm through the narrow gap. His fingers located the bolt. He drew it back, yanked the door open, ran out onto the small landing, and began to go downstairs.

Even before reaching the level below, he was forced to stop. He could feel the heat, see the red glow, smell to the point of nausea the smoke, which was billowing lazily toward him.

He charged back up. The other door above was as firmly locked as previously. Going into the room, he crossed to the window. Its catch was broken. He saw, in any case, that the frame had long ago been nailed closed; cobwebs and rusty nailheads told the story.

Apple stood back, raised his leg, and kicked at the glass. It went tinkling out. There were two crosspieces of wood that he also kicked free.

Apple was aware of a sudden increase in the fire's elements. He could hear the crackle. In breaking the window, he realized, he had created a chimney. He should have closed the door first. Now he had less time than before.

Quickly he worked at wriggling shards from the frame. That done, he leaned out. He had the attention of everyone below. People began shouting advice, firemen gave contradictory orders. Everyone, obviously, had believed the building to be empty.

Several of the firemen ran toward a truck that was parked further along the street. It had a ladder on a turntable. But there were other vehicles that would have to be moved out of the way first. And the heat was getting closer.

Apple breathed smoke. It sent him into a paroxysm of coughing. He thought it would never stop. To get clean air he leaned far out and aside. Lungs clearing, he blinked tears from his eyes and looked up behind him. The metal guttering appeared to be fairly strong.

Turning, Apple shuffled cautiously into a sit on the windowsill. He reached up with one hand. If he had been two inches shorter, he would never have made it. He was able to curl his fingers over the gutter's edge. That grip firm, he stretched up the other arm, and again got a solid hold.

Apple pulled on the gutter. There was no give. Slowly, he brought his lower body through the window until he was fully outside and standing in a squat on the sill, then moved erect so that he was upright and above the eaves.

There he paused to take stock of the situation. He refused to hurry despite the heat on his legs.

He had, he saw, two choices. He could try to crawl up onto the roof, which was sickeningly steep, and get over to the next house (there was no break between buildings); he could let himself hang down from his grip and hand-walk along to the window next door.

The second choice offered the most dangers, Apple thought: the gutter breaking, his arms running out of power, his fingers unable to support the weight. It would have to be the first.

Delicately, Apple leaned forward onto the tiles. Wishing

the crowd would make less clamour, he took his left hand off the gutter and reached it ahead as far as he could. He got a feeble grip on the corner of a tile.

Stomach quaking, he began to raise his left leg. He brought it over the guttering and onto the roof. Slowly he inched forward onto his belly, feeling the terror of needing to let go of his other foothold. It felt even worse when he had to take his right hand off the gutter. He compensated by lying his cheek flat to the tiles.

Gradually Apple forged upward, away from the eaves. He took pinch grips on tile corners. He didn't hurry as smoke began to curl up through the roof. He kept his gaze firmly on its apex.

Which he reached at last, and grabbed on to with love. Faster now, he hauled himself up into a straddle on the point. Not looking to either side, he sat his way along to the next roof, then the next.

There, a skylight rose into the air. A head appeared, an arm waved.

Apple let himself down from the apex on his face. Limbs spread like a star, he edged toward the skylight. The fact that he was annoyed by the way the gun poked his stomach told him that his fear had gone. He was safe now.

One minute later, Apple was being helped down onto a chair that stood on a table. The attic was full of people. Some were in uniform—firemen and policemen. Only one face was familiar. It belonged to Captain Domingo Sanchez.

Somehow, he wasn't quite sure how he did it, Apple managed to avoid the Civil Guard officer when he reached the floor; managed to edge through the backslappers to the door. More people were lining the stairway.

Apple forged on by, wearing a grin. That was not how he

was feeling. Relief at escape fading, the pain in his head was making itself known again and he was realizing that, probably, someone had tried to kill him.

He heard Captain Sanchez calling his name. He hurried, being less gentle with the people who stood in his way, no longer acting a grin and ignoring the hands offered for shaking.

Apple came to the ground floor. He pushed through the mob to the building's rear and went outside. The yard was deserted. He crossed it, came out into an alley, and charged along it to the street. Circling, he reached his rented car.

Slamming inside, Apple started the motor. Ahead in the deepening dusk he saw the form of Captain Sanchez. Apple sent the 2CV surging forward and into a U-turn. The yellow body tilted to its limits and the front wheels stammered in protest; but the car made it around.

Switching the lights on, Apple turned again at the first corner. He put his foot to the floor, screaming along in second gear. That feeling of urgency was back in full force.

Apple kept on the same street. After several blocks, no new pairs of lights coming into sight in the rearview mirror, he knew he had got cleanly away from Domingo Sanchez.

It wasn't until he had driven for five minutes, taking different directions, that Apple found his bearings. He headed for the main road. Another five minutes and he was turning into the lane beside the walled villa.

Switching off motor and headlights, he picked up his flash and got out of the car. He used its front wing as a step to get his hands on top of the wall. The rest was simple. He let himself down easily on the other side.

Lighted windows showed dimly through the trees, presenting a picture that was more romantic than sinister. Irked at that, Apple went forward at a pace which he part-knew to be unnecessarily cautious.

He held the lit flash in his left hand and played its beam only a little way ahead. He was wondering what he would do if a whole pack of dogs came charging at him. Such a possibility hadn't been broached in Training Two.

Apple got a boost from realizing that his headache had eased and his mouth had stopped tasting like a workhouse floor. He was, in fact, feeling pretty good. This could be due to his escape from the fire, he mused, or to his still being slightly drunk.

He saw the dog. It was standing directly in his path as he rounded the thick trunk of a tree. He came to a stop and eased and his mouth had stopped tasting like a workhouse before.

Like last night, the tall thin gingery dog was perfectly still. Its teeth were again out on show. Unblinking and silent it stared up at Apple menacingly.

They were separated by six feet. Apple reduced this a little as now, tensely, he went into action. He leaned forward and stuck out his right forearm.

Nothing happened.

According to theory, the dog should have leapt for the arm with a snarl. Instead, it remained quiet and motionless.

Apple tried again. Crouching in a threatening manner, he jabbed forward with his arm bent and grated, "Sic it, you brute."

The Podenco Ibizenco made no response. Nor was there any change when Apple tried a third time, and even took a step forward. The animal was not about to cooperate. Apple straightened with a sigh.

After a moment, feeling tired, not able to go forward and

unwilling to go back, he sank to a squat. He said in a low, weary voice, "This isn't getting us anywhere."

The dog's ears twitched.

Encouraged, Apple went on, "You see, what I want to do is get to the house there. Don't ask me why. It's a sort of instinct, I imagine. I feel that that's where the answer is. You know what I mean?"

A change came over the Podenco Ibizenco's long muzzle. Some seconds passed before Apple realized that the gleaming teeth were hidden from view. In a friendly tone he said, "My name's Arnold. Well, it isn't really, but names aren't all that important. I'm sure you feel the same. What *is* important, at least to me, is that I go to the villa. I've been doing so badly on this mission. If I flop, I might never get another. And they matter to me. Greatly."

The dog put its head on one side.

Apple said, "Not, mind you, that I'd be desperately unhappy without them. I do have my other work, after all." He went on to tell of the United Kingdom Philological Society; next about his apartment in Bloomsbury; next of Hyde Park, where he often went walking.

Slowly, the dog's tail swung one way, then the other, then came back to the central position. A wag had been performed.

"Well now," Apple said. "There we are."

The dog shifted its head to a tilt on the opposite side. Its gaze was still on Apple's face, though with the fixedness gone. There were occasional blinks, like punctuation.

Not sinking to sloppy-cute speech, knowing better than to talk down to a dog, Apple went on with the subject of Hyde Park. He mentioned that it covered three hundred and eighty-eight acres, that many duels had been fought there, including one between Samuel Martin and John Wilkes in 1763, and that Rotten Row was a corruption of *Route de Roi*.

Lowering its head, the dog came forward at a casual amble. After moving around so that it was facing the same way as Apple, it sat down at his side. They languidly turned on one another the same look, one that was calm and sympathetic.

Apple nodded several times before saying, "That's better. Now we're pals. But I don't know your name. So what I'll do is give you one. All right?"

The long tail flopped once against the grass. Apple said, "Good. In that case let's think about it. There're lots of good names. For instance we have . . ."

While pronouncing at a steady speed whatever name came into his head, be it first or last or place, he raised his hand slowly toward the muzzle.

"Jenkins . . . Jack . . . Sprat . . . Billingsgate . . ." he said as the dog sniffed his hand; "Bristol . . . Carl . . . Ernest . . ." as he trailed his fingers along the furry jowl; "Norman . . . March . . ." as gently he began to stroke the top of the head.

Breathing out a little sigh, Apple concluded, "I'll call you Monico. It's the sort of masculine version of monicker. Okay? Good."

He took his hand away and rose. "Care to stroll, Monico?"

The house was medium to large in size, on two floors and painted white. There was a terrace ten feet broad that looked to go all the way around the building; it rose a yard above the surrounding grass, with its low wall broken at regular intervals where steps led down. There were lit windows on both levels.

Side by side, Apple and Monico approached through the

trees. Apple had switched off his flash. The risk was greater than the need: the house being white was a great help to visibility.

Apple was thinking that he certainly must be still slightly drunk, otherwise he would be feeling surprised at having won the dog over. As it was, he had accepted the fact with ease. He wondered if he owned some latent gift, a power over animals, that only now was beginning to emerge.

That kept Apple's mind off danger as he covered the last few yards. He stopped by one of the short flights of steps. With Monico standing beside him, he listened. There was nothing to be heard, either hereabouts or from inside, the lit but curtained windows as mute as the black ones.

It was the latter that Apple had feared during his approach. They, he had thought, could easily be hiding a guard with a rifle. Even though he told himself he was dramatizing, he felt safer now that he had arrived.

Looking down at the dog, Apple made a firm staying gesture with a flattened hand and ordered softly, "Wait here." He nodded and went up the steps. Monico followed.

And stopped when Apple did, which happened as soon as he was on the flagstone terrace. He bent low to whisper, "No. You stay." The dog blinked at him affectionately. It followed when Apple took two long, crouching steps backwards, gave a tail wag in answer to a shaken finger.

Opting for a different attitude, reason instead of command, Apple offered both hands with a murmured "I want you to try and see the situation from my point of view, old man."

Monico lifted a front leg and laid its paw on one of the reasoning hands. Apple gave up. After shaking the paw politely he rose and turned away. The dog followed.

Apple went to the nearest window. The curtains, glowing from a lamp inside, were an inch away from meeting in the middle. Through the crack Apple could see a small library. It was deserted. He moved on.

The next two windows were dark. The next, around a corner of the house, was bright with light, its curtains drawn back. Apple was cautious about peering in. But the room, a scullery, held only stores and kitchen equipment.

Even so, Apple kept up his caution, ducking under the window to go on by. He didn't care for the silence of the place. No occupied house should be so dead.

He came to the front door. There were broad steps here leading down from the terrace. On a fronting turnabout, bulbous end of the driveway, stood two cars. They were average in size, grey in colour.

With Monico closely behind, Apple went over to the cars. He tried the door handles. They were firm. He returned to the terrace and went on with his snooping.

It was around the next corner that he saw the french windows. They sent onto the flagstones a tall oblong of yellow, like luminous paint. There were no drawn curtains to hinder light, or to contain sound, such as the one that came now: a man clearing his throat.

Caution increased, Apple moved close to the wall. He took his time about reaching the french windows. Another brief session of throat-clearing came as he stopped. He got down on one knee to edge his head around until he could see inside.

The room came slowly into view. It was cheaply and sparingly furnished. No rugs lay on the tiled floor. The mantelpiece mirror had adhesive tape over the cracks in each corner. The feebly framed pictures had been conceived in a factory and birthed in a chain store. It was the kind of room that tourists expect, and usually get, when they rent a property on a weekly or monthly basis.

Apple held his panning observation on seeing the man. He

was in profile, sitting on an upright chair, leaning forward over his crossed legs. His hair was long, his Zapata moustache . . .

Apple nodded with satisfaction. He was pleased to find Hippie here. It made things neat. Surprises were always disturbing.

Something cold and wet landed behind Apple's left ear. He jerked forward and almost overbalanced. For perhaps three seconds he was in full view of anyone inside the room. He didn't look to find out, but worked at getting himself back.

In shadow, he waited. As nothing happened, he knew that Hippie hadn't glanced around. Wiping where the dog's nose had touched, Apple whispered over his shoulder, "Don't do that again."

For safety, he got onto his hands and knees before returning to his careful observation. His scanning eyes passed Hippie, passed another stretch of wall with a Woolworth landscape, and came to a couch. On the couch lay a man. He was on his side and faced the other way.

Apple frowned. He thought there was something familiar about those shoulders and the back of that head, though the hair and the dark suit told him nothing. After a minute of watching, Apple felt that he must be mistaken.

He panned on, saw the rest of the gaunt room, came back to the man on the couch, who was under the morose gaze of Hippie. Again Apple was taken by a sense of recognition.

Hippie cleared his throat. The lying man stirred and raised his head, then settled back. Apple had seen the side of his face. The man was Angus Watkin.

After crawling backwards until he was well clear of the french windows, Apple got up. He went on to the corner of the house, stepped around it, and leaned on the wall. He was filled with the weariness of shock.

While his mind worked at trying to absorb the fact that his superior in British Intelligence was being held prisoner in the villa, it also had a stab at making sense of the whole Ibiza situation. It had little enthusiasm for either project, for one was as crazy as the other.

What if no one at the pension was involved in the KGB's drug game? Could be that it was simply the contact point, and as such was constantly under observation, by Hippie and others, who made a careful check of all who came to stay.

Looking down at the dog, where it sat close at hand, Apple shook his head. It didn't wash, he thought, because of Hippie and Maria having taken Jason Lock to the clinic. Unless, of course, Lock was part of the team, contact man on the premises, or there to be on the lookout for snoopers.

Apple nodded. That washed, he told Monico silently. Lock had suspected Arnold Barker and had called in a Sickle— Maria Sola. She and Hippie had rescued the supposed ex-dentist . . .

In that case, Apple wondered, who had been responsible for Jason Lock's injury? Could there be undercover agents from other countries involved?

Apple pushed himself off the wall. His mind, he decided, was in no shape to go into complexities. But what it would have to do was come up with an idea for securing Angus Watkin's release. And as soon as possible.

To Apple occurred the idea of going to Captain Sanchez. That, however, was out of the question. The very last person you went to on a mission was a policeman, even in your own country.

Apple concluded that he had to get inside the house.

Followed by Monico, he went to a window, which he examined with a lot of touch and minimum sight. He found that there would be no way of making an entry without also making noise.

Going on, Apple made a circuit of the building. All windows were firm and beyond his basic knowledge of burglary. He finished up by the front door.

He could always knock, he thought, and use his gun to hold up whoever answered. But there might be a secret peephole, or they might come at him from around the sides.

He could draw them out by making the horn blast continually on one of the cars—breaking in and crossing the pertinent wires would be a simple matter. But the very fact of the blasting would let them know that something was wrong, thus destroying his one advantage.

He could climb up on the roof and hope for a skylight. But there might not be one, and if he made a noise, if they came out, he'd be a sitting duck up there.

The only way was a surprise attack.

Apple went back to the french windows. Kneeling, he looked first at the frames. He saw with satisfaction that they were of slender wood, old and flimsy to boot. Next he peeped inside.

The scene was the same. Hippie sat on his straight-backed chair stolidly watching the couch, which was about eight feet away. Angus Watkin lay perfectly still.

Apple thought attack while continuing to watch.

From somewhere inside his multicoloured clothing, Hippie brought out a pack of cigarettes.

Now, Apple urged himself. This is the moment to rush in. But then he remembered a segment from Training Three. The pedantic instructor had said: "There are four occasions when a conscious person is totally out of touch with his surroundings. These are, starting with that of the longest duration: during sexual climax, while yawning, when sneezing, and throughout the act of drawing in the first inhalation of smoke from a newly lit cigarette."

Right, Apple thought. He backed off, got up, patted Monico briefly, and went to the low wall. From there he jumped down to the grass. After putting down the flashlight he brought out his gun and snicked off the safety catch.

Opposite the french windows were steps. Apple stood back from them and looked directly into the room. Hippie, a cigarette in his lips, was putting the pack away. Apple felt stupid at experiencing a tingle of desire in his mouth.

Hippie patted his clothing. It seemed to take for ever for him to find the right place. He delved into it and produced a lighter. He flicked it on, put flame to cigarette.

Apple burst from his taut stance. He charged to the steps and up, leapt across the terrace, flung himself right shoulder first at the french windows.

They burst open with a tremendous crash. Inside, as he spilled forward into a fall, which he was unable to prevent, Apple was aware of a cry of alarm and the tinkle of falling glass.

He hit the floor. As he did, the gun jumped from his hand. But Apple was sliding in the same direction on the tiles, and with a great, convulsive snatch, he managed to grab the gun while it was still in the air.

Lying prone, the slide over, he swung his upper body to the left. He was just in time to see Hippie disappearing behind a wing chair. Apple jerked around to face the other way.

Angus Watkin was settling himself from having sat up. Face as bland as always, he clasped his hands together and leaned forward. "What on earth," he said, "are you playing at?"

His name was Tom Brown. He was in school, at Rugby. Several of his classmates, led by Flashman, were holding him bent double. His buttocks were being forced closer and closer to the blazing log fire.

The ploy worked. The heat drained from Apple's face, which, to his relief, was half hidden by being directed toward the tiles, thus making the blush less noticeable. He rolled over and sat up. The floor felt warm.

Watkin asked, "Are you all right, Porter?"

"Yes, sir. Thank you."

"I trust that your gun is quite safe."

Apple snicked on the catch and put the revolver back behind his belt. When he looked up again, it was to see Angus Watkin gesturing toward the wing chair, with "Allow me to introduce you to Agent Eleven."

Hippie was sinking back into the chair with a tense movement. He gave a brusque nod. His features were no more seeable than before behind the moustache and dangling hair.

The need-to-view rule as applied to underlings like me, Apple thought as he returned the nod with equal coolness. He said, "How do you do."

"Hello."

"You made a neat job of getting old Lock out of that pit."

The Zapata moustache twitched. Angus Watkin, undrawn, said, "And this other gentleman you have already met."

Turning the other way, Apple saw, in a corner doorway, the car-snob operative he knew as Fourteen. He was casually putting a revolver into a shoulder holster.

"Hello again, Six," he said. "I thought the roof had fallen in or something."

"Hello. I suppose I did make a bit of a racket."

Coldly, his tone a rebuke for their daring to exchange chat, Angus Watkin said, "The windows, Fourteen, if you would be so kind."

The operative went to the french windows and squeaked them closed. Before he drew the curtains, Apple caught a dim glimpse of the dog. Monico was sitting patiently in the penumbra.

"Thank you, Fourteen," Watkin said. "That will be all. See to it that we get some tea, mm?"

His face taut at the dismissal, Fourteen silently left the room and silently closed the door behind him. Apple sympathized.

He said to his superior, "I'm sorry, sir, for bursting in on you like this. The fact is, I thought you were being held prisoner."

"And you wanted to save me, Porter?" He sounded bored. "That was considerate of you. However, I'm sure there must have been some other way you could have gone about it."

"Perhaps, sir," Apple mumbled. He told himself he might have known there would be no appreciation of his good intentions, the possible sacrifice of his life.

"But let us not make a big issue out of the damage to the property, Porter. Possibly Accounts can afford the expense. And, since you are here, I might as well fill you in on what's been happening."

"Yes, sir. Thank you."

"Please be seated. Properly."

Apple got off the floor, which had cooled, lifted the upright chair from where it had fallen when vacated by Hippie, and sat. He said, so as not to appear completely in the dark, "What's Maria Sola's number name in this operation, sir?"

"Sixteen," Angus Watkin said, grudgingly, and Apple was

amused at the man's childishness. Obviously he had wanted Maria's role to come as a surprise. "You saw her with Eleven, of course, taking Mr. Lock to the clinic."

"Yes, sir."

"Before that, you suspected nothing. She had an awful time trying to get you in the right place, so that you could be picked up by Fourteen, so that he, in turn, could bring you to see me in the helicopter."

Apple nodded, remembering the necking session on the housing development, the other car, the chase. He longed to say that he had suspected then, but that wouldn't do Maria any good.

"Now to the nub," Angus Watkin said, leaning back on the couch. "Starting with George Trent. We didn't know who had dealt with him, so you were sent in to find out. That much you are aware of."

"Yes, sir," Apple said cheerfully.

"What you are possibly not aware of, Porter, is method. Ours, not yours. In the trade it's usually referred to as the Invitation Waltz. In other words, the best way to draw someone from behind a mask is to take off one's own. Therefore it was decided to let the villain suspect Arnold Barker. Clear?"

Apple nodded, but without cheer. That had gone. Inside him he felt the beginnings of a chill.

Watkin said, "So it was fixed for you to arrive in the same way as George Trent—by boat, after a cable had been sent. The arrangement is just that bit rare enough to be possibly more than a coincidence, to a suspicious mind. It seemed to work, for within minutes of your arrival there was that near-miss business with the car."

Apple's chill continued to spread.

"To help the Invitation Waltz further," his superior went on, "we left certain gaps when briefing you on your cover—

how you came to choose the Royal Rose, for example—so that you would have to rely on invention. Hopefully, the lies would be seen through."

And Appleton Porter scores 6 out of 10 in ability to invent, Apple mused grimly. He could feel the chill growing.

Angus Watkin said, "We couldn't go too far because we didn't want Moscow to know that we, the Service, were in any way involved. You were to be taken for a friend of Trent's, investigating his disappearance, or a policeman doing the same."

Apple, chilled, thought: And that long drink of water Appleton Porter fitted the bill perfectly, as being someone who was most unlikely to be used as an espionage operative.

"The car thing we knew about at once," Watkin went on. "But other attempts on your health—the scorpion and the falling plant pot—were unknown to us until you told me of them in the helicopter. Therefore we needed to give more hints that you spelled trouble.

"Agent Sixteen was sent in. She took the Trent page from the ledger and put it in your room. The hope was that word of it would get to the right person. You, however, found it yourself, and put it under Jason Lock's door. That, it seemed, was a dead end. Are you following all this, Porter?"

"Avidly," Apple said. He realized that the chill had crept into his voice.

"We, and you, know about the wind-surfer mast that nearly hit you. But there were two other attempts of which you were probably unaware. One was a glass of poisoned fruit juice. For some reason, perhaps instinct, you emptied it into a plant pot."

Apple, playing the bumbling amateur, said stolidly, "I did it because I don't like juices. They curdle my stomach."

Angus Watkin flicked him a sharp glance before saying,

"The plant died, you might care to know, though analysis of the soil was inconclusive as to whether or not the dose would have been lethal to a human."

Not that you'd have minded, Apple thought, his chill making itself known as hate and rage.

Watkin: "Also there was the matter of the rose. The one left on your pillow. It was saturated with an anesthetic. You did not, it appears, smell it, but took it downstairs."

Apple said nothing. He was busy keeping his feelings hidden.

"Even so," Angus Watkin went on, "we didn't know who was responsible for all this. More hints needed to be given. So an imitation identity card was left in your room by Sixteen. It said that you were with Scotland Yard."

"Imitation?" Apple said. "The Yard cleared it as genuine."

"They were doing us a favour," Watkin said. He gave a small, bored-seeming sigh. "They owe us so many."

From Hippie came a grunt that might have been a laugh. Apple forced himself to smile, play along.

Watkin: "You failed to mention the card, Porter, when we met."

"Did I? It must have slipped my mind."

"Anyway, the card apparently stirred things up. Though it did us no particular good." He turned his head as the corner door opened. Maria came in with a tray, and Watkin's face took on a tinge of warmth, a near-animation.

"Ah," he said. "Tea."

Maria put her tray on a table by the couch end. She wore a plain dress that reached down primly beyond her knees and up severely to her throat, flat shoes, no cosmetics, a peasant-style scarf that covered her hair.

This was a Maria that Apple hadn't seen before. Not that

he was seeing the new one, not completely. The difference, the details, he registered automatically. It was something for him to do with his eyes.

Apple's chill had faded, been digested. He had a dull, quiet anger. But he hoped it was invisible from the outside.

Invitation Waltz, he thought. That was a pleasant term for a sick situation. The true analogy was the goat-to-catch-tiger routine used by white hunters. You tied a goat to a stake in a clearing. Around it were covered pits, into which the tiger was supposed to fall, unharmed, when drawn by the goat's bleating. Except that more often than not, wily tiger avoided the pits and had a free supper.

And he was the goat, Apple mused. It was hardly surprising that Watkin hadn't been impressed by his believing he was risking his life by bursting in here. He had been risking his life for days. He had been waiting on the sacrificial altar, an offering to the greater glory of Angus Watkin, who had calmly hoped for the villain to unmask himself by making an all-out attempt to destroy the suspected guest.

Apple realized he was shaking his head. He stopped it and sat straighter, became more alert to externals.

Maria had served Watkin. She took a cup to Hippie and returned to the table, her walk another switch from the broad to the narrow. She looked at Apple: "It's two sugars, isn't it, Six?" The only accent in her English had been born in Mayfair, between silk sheets.

"Yes, please, Maria. I'll go on calling you that, if you don't mind." He was putting on a good performance, he assured himself.

Maria said, "Actually, I rather like the name."

"It has a bit more going for it than Sixteen."

"Oh, absolutely."

"Thanks, by the way," Apple said, "for helping me out

with the gun when Captain Sanchez was there. It must've been you."

"Yes. I palmed it off the table and put it in your room later."

Angus Watkin cleared his throat.

Maria served Apple, got a cup for herself, and sat on the couch. As if by training, her hemline fell of its own accord to a position that allowed no hint of knees.

Watkin asked her, "Is the detainee conscious?"

"Yes, sir."

"Good. We'll get around to that after we've had our tea." He looked at Apple over his cup. "She suffered a slight blow on the head while she was being persuaded to come along here. She proved quite agile, it seems."

Apple must have shown the question on his face, for Watkin added, "Yes, Porter, the villain is a lady."

To save himself from having to answer, or comment, Apple took a long drink.

After a moment Angus Watkin said, "You're probably curious about Jason Lock's involvement in this. It was incidental. Though extremely nosy—out of boredom, one imagines—he's a harmless fellow, as is that colonial, whatsisname."

"Harry Lewis," Apple supplied obediently, while aware that his chief knew the man's name perfectly well.

"Quite so. However, Mr. Lock came into it through the misplaced initiative of Agent Sixteen." He gave a faint smile.

Evidently taking the pause for permission to speak, Maria said tonelessly, "I believe I told you, sir, that I thought there was no connection with the mission, that it would be a complication that we could well do without. I was wrong, of course."

As if she hadn't spoken, a trick familiar to Apple from his

own experiences with his superior, Watkin said, "And how did you, Porter, happen to be in on that particular development?"

Apple told of feeling that he had to search somewhere for the missing ex-dentist and deciding to start with the sandstone quarry. "I followed Maria and Eleven to the clinic, and then on to the house here. Or at least, to the gate."

Watkin said, "They didn't know they were being followed," which for him was top praise. But next came "The walls were too high for you, perhaps?"

"I had the suspicion—a faint one, admittedly—that the pair could be on our side. I decided to leave it like that for the time being."

The way Angus Watkin asked for more tea showed that he took the excuse as a lie. When his cup had been refilled he said, "What happened was, the lady gave a message to Sixteen to pass on to you, Porter, but saying it had come from somebody else. A neat enough trick."

Loving every word, Apple said, "Then the message must have been verbal, sir."

"Which I stated, I think."

"Perhaps I misheard." He spoke heavily, to show that he was merely being diplomatic.

Bland as ever, Angus Watkin sipped his tea. He said, "The message was for you to meet sender at the quarry. Sixteen, as we already know, gave the message instead to Jason Lock. I suppose he played along because of having had that ledger page pushed under his door, whereas normally of course he would have gone directly to source.

"Still, he got a taxi and went. Seeing him arrive, the lady naturally assumed that he was involved with you. The thing almost becomes a comedy of errors. She gave him a crack on the skull with a rock and left him for dead. But he was alive when Sixteen got there—she in the interim having had second thoughts in the matter."

The way Watkin passed his cup to Maria for her to put it on the table was as though he were giving her a gift, a present for her second thoughts. He said, "Sixteen went back for Eleven, to help carry Lock down and take him to a clinic. As the matter turned out, it was not a mere nuisance. We were able to turn it to our advantage. With it we laid our final persuasion. We telephoned the pension and left a message for you, Porter, supposedly from Mr. Lock. The gist was that he, having recovered consciousness, urged you to go to see him because he wanted to tell you who had hit him at the quarry. That, of course, did the trick. The lady got you drunk, took you up to the attic, locked you in, and set fire to the building."

Apple nodded. "That much is obvious."

"The lady had come out from behind her mask. She was on her way to the clinic, to deal with Jason Lock, when she was taken into custody." He turned toward Maria. "All right, Sixteen. Let's have the lady in."

As Maria got up and came to collect cups, Watkin said, "And if you, Porter, open your mouth once during the forthcoming interview, you will regret it for the rest of your life."

Apple believed him. From now on, he would believe Angus Watkin to be capable of anything.

Which, some minutes later, didn't prevent Apple from being initially shocked, drawn forward into a lean of surprise, on hearing the sharp tones of London's East End issue from his superior's mouth.

"Okay," Watkin said over his shoulder as the door opened, "get yourself in here and sharp about it."

Oddly, Apple was less startled to see Mona; to realize that she was the villain; to know that she was a Sickle—female agent for the KGB. He felt more disappointment than surprise.

After Maria had retreated and closed the door, Mona hesitated on the threshold. She wore jeans and a crumpled shirt. Her face was pale except for a red patch on the right cheek, close to the ear (Apple knew about that particular blow). Defiance was trying to subdue the standard expression of concern.

She asked, "What's all this about?"

"Going to play it that way, are we?" Watkin said. "Come and sit here, girlie, or you might get another tap on the loaf."

Apple acknowledged that it was well done, though he was mystified as to the reason for the Cockney tough-guy impersonation. He avoided looking directly at Mona as she came around and sat on the couch, at the opposite end from Watkin, who had pointed out the place with a severe finger.

"You know who we are, right enough," Angus Watkin said. "But maybe you think we don't know who *you* are."

Mona looked at him warily. "I don't understand you. Not in the least. I do not know who you people are. I'd like an explanation. It must be a joke. I—" She broke off as Watkin made a curt gesture.

In matching tone he said, "Never mind, girlie. Forget it. To show you what a sweet guy I am we'll play it your way. I'll spell it out for you. Then maybe you'll drop the curtain on this act. Eh?"

Not answering, Mona wrapped a fist around each plait end and brought it to meet the other on her chest. She looked down at her faded jeans. The defiance had gone. Sharing the expression of worry now was puzzlement.

"We," Angus Watkin said, "are businessmen. We operate

all over Europe. A multinational corporation, you might say, except we don't keep no books and we ain't got no offices and you won't find us quoted on the stock exchange. The product we sell is peace of mind. It's for people what otherwise would be real unhappy. Am I right, Jack?"

"Right," Hippie said. They both laughed.

As Watkin talked on in similar facetious vein, Apple got the picture. His superior was presenting himself as a gangster, part of a big-time organization. This was so the KGB wouldn't know about the involvement of British Intelligence.

Finishing with another laugh, which Hippie shared, Angus Watkin asked, "Clear enough for you, girlie?"

Still looking down, Mona nodded. "I think so. But I—"

"Christ," Watkin said, as if bored. "Don't overdo it. I could get very pissed off with you. And when I'm that way, I'm nasty. Am I right, Jack?"

"Right," Hippie said. There was no laugh.

Watkin folded his arms. "I'll do some more spelling. I'll tell you who you are, in case you've forgotten. Never can tell, you might've been dipping into the goods as they passed through."

Mona said, "You're not making sense."

"Sure I am, girlie. By goods I mean acid, coke, and horse. Though I dare say they have different terms for 'em in Moscow."

She shot him a fast, oblique glance. He went on, "Yes, dear, we know the whole bit. We've done a lot of poking into this little scene. We haven't got your real name but we know you're a Russki and that you work for the spy people, the KGB."

Mona gave herself away by becoming still and expressionless. Her performance, to Watkin's, was like an amateur's next to that of a grand old trouper.

"Sorry I don't speak the Russki lingo," Watkin said. "But you do okay with English. Okay enough to get my meaning."

Mona shook her head. "I don't understand a thing. I want you to let me go."

"We will, girlie, we *will*. I told you I was a sweet guy, didn't I? But we got to get a few points settled. See, we're going to take over this operation. That's a lovely bit of stuff you people're running. It goes to the States, I reckon, but we have a nice market for it in Britain and elsewhere. Am I right, Jack?"

"Right," Hippie said. "So we want to know about the incoming connection. How it gets out of here don't interest us."

Angus Watkin nodded. "We want the supplier. He'll switch to us, all right. Money talks every language, as me dear old granny used to say. And, as I say, muscle talks fastest. I think you're with me now, dear."

Mona looked at him while painting her underchin with the brush ends of both plaits. She said, "No, I'm not."

Watkin smiled, as if with reluctant admiration. "Come on, kid. We *know* about you. You gave yourself away. You did it by getting rid of George Trent and by working at doing the same with poor old Arnold here. They was only trying to get at the facts without pushing. But you was closed up tight. There was too many other silly bastards nosing around, for no good reason, like that Lock and his part-time sidekick Mrs. Arkwright. Yes, girlie, you gave yourself away, so you might as well ring down the curtain."

Mona brought back the expression of puzzlement. She asked, "Gave myself away?" Her acting was deteriorating.

Where earlier Apple had experienced the beginnings of a chill, now he felt the faint start of a warmth.

"Me, I'm a great speller," Angus Watkin said. "So let's begin with that nonsense with the car, eh? To do the hit-and-run bit you hired some sleazy guy from Argentina. Afterwards he crawled back under his rock, but we finally got him out of there."

The last bit was a bluff, Apple judged, though he could see that it was working.

"Everything would've worked out fine, girlie, if you'd pushed old Arnold just the right amount. Unfortunately for you, you shoved him so hard he went right across the street, and the car missed him."

As Apple's warmth continued to grow, Mona looked down again and slowly started to paint the side of her face. She had given up on the puzzlement. Feebly she muttered, "What nonsense."

Angus Watkin said, "Next you had a bash with that scorpion. But it didn't come off, mainly because you'd tied a bloody great knot in what should've looked like a spider's thread. So no go."

Watkin nodded. "The plant pot. Now that was a cunning little idea, girlie, I'll grant you that. You fastened the wool to the pot before you sat at the patio table with old Arnold to do a bit of knitting. But you must've forgot that wool stretches. By the time you'd finished pulling, it was too late."

Apple blinked as the warmth came up behind his eyes. Mona's own eyes, he noted, were tinged with heat.

"Then there was that business with the poison," Watkin said. "You put it in the fruit juice. Problem was, you didn't take the trouble to find out first if your guest *liked* juices. He don't."

Hippie said, "It must've tasted rotten anyway. Christ."

Angus Watkin went on, "I think the wind-surfer bit came next. You got it to fall okay, dear, and without letting yourself be seen, but it hit the wrong person, *and* without doing any real damage.

"Another flop was the rose, though again, a neat idea. But

Arnold didn't sniff it and get a dose of the anesthetic. He put it in the vase on the lobby desk. The only one to be overcome, girlie, was you."

Apple recalled the fainting spell. His warmth thrived.

"And the last bit," Watkin said, "was getting Arnold drunk and putting him upstairs. What you didn't know was that people who're quickly affected by booze, they recover quickly. You thought he'd be out for hours, I reckon. That's why you didn't do your worst while you had him helpless. The fire, you thought, would take care of everything. And we saw you setting that fire. In fact, I can still smell the petrol on you."

The detainee's eyes sadly roamed the floor—and Apple's warmth came firmly into possession of his spirits. He accepted the truth about Mona. She was a bumbler. She was a low-rung operative. She was a faceless one.

What Apple was realizing, without actually thinking, was that Mona Smith was a female, Russian version of Appleton Porter.

With not the slightest conviction, Mona said, "I was filling a lighter and spilled the fluid on myself."

Angus Watkin nodded again, happily. "Course you did. Me, I'll believe anything. I'd believe the moon was made of mousetraps. Right, Jack?"

"Right," Hippie said. They shared a laugh. There was no humour in it.

Watkin pointed along the couch. "Listen, girlie. Get it into your head that we know about you. Even if it wasn't for all those little bitty things I mentioned, there's something else."

Apple noted that his superior wasn't bothering to try and explain away the Yard Card. Maybe he thought it wasn't necessary with someone of a faceless one's ilk.

Mona asked, "What something else?"

"We got the word on you from George Trent."

She shot him a glance. It held a glimmer of hope. Releasing the plaits, she folded her arms and said, "I still haven't the faintest idea what you're talking about. Whoever you are."

Angus Watkin gave a cheerful sigh. Even inside the impersonation his pleasure was apparent to Apple, who sat straighter and firmly folded his arms.

Watkin said a light "I know a way to make you own up, drop the curtain, stop wasting our time. Several ways, in fact." He looked across the room. "Let's start with the first, eh, Jack?"

Hippie got up. Mona tensed, and Apple became aware of his own sudden tension. Is this, he thought, where the muscle begins? But Hippie came by him from behind and, followed intently by Mona's eyes, went past the couch and over to the door, which he opened. He leaned out, upper body hidden. There was a murmur of voices.

Her face in semi-profile, Mona shot her gaze to Apple. They looked steadily at each other until a movement at the door made them turn that way.

A man came in. He was about thirty, average height and build. His face was also average. The only factors out of the ordinary about him were his dressing gown and the bandage taped to one side of his head, where the hair had been shaved.

Angus Watkin said, "I'm sure, girlie, that you won't have forgotten George Trent."

After a moment of silence the man, solemn, said, "Hello, Mona."

Her face sad, slack, tired, Mona turned back to face front.

It was a good piece of Watkin theatre, Apple conceded, and of course the man was undoubtedly the operative who had been going under the name of George Trent, another of Mona's failures. But equally clear was the fact that Trent had not been able to pinpoint the villain, otherwise there would have been no need to send in Appleton Porter to play Invitation Waltz.

Apple thought this while staring at Mona's brow.

Watkin said, "Okay, George. Back to your rest."

The operative went quietly out. Hippie closed the door and leaned back on it. There was another silence. It ended at last when Angus Watkin asked, "Is the curtain still up, girlie, or have you finally come to your senses?"

Mona offered no reply, either by word or by gesture. She took her left plait in both hands and stared drably at the floor. The ploy had worked, her attitude stated. She was admitting by the fact of no longer denying.

Watkin said, "So, Miss KGB, now that we've got that settled, let's have no more nonsense. I want you to tell me how the stuff comes in."

Mona still had nothing to say. She didn't even shake her head when Angus Watkin asked, "Are you going to tell me?" It looked as if she had drifted into a sad daydream. Her eyes did, however, become more alert in response to "I can make you talk, y'know." Obviously, she believed he was prepared to use torture.

Apple believed the same. Sweat tickled in his armpits.

Watkin said, "I'll ask one more time. Just one. How does the stuff come in?"

Apple eased his body forward, toward Mona, urging her to speak. She stayed as still and silent as before.

Now there was no cheeriness in Angus Watkin's sigh. He gazed around the room, glanced at Hippie and looked at Apple, who straightened abruptly, almost guiltily. Watkin gave a slow nod.

"Girlie," he said, "before we start to slap your wrist, I'll give you a last chance. I'll let old Arnold here talk to you. Alone. He knows you and I don't. Maybe he can make you see the light. If that doesn't work—too bad. You can't blame me. I tried to do it the nice way. I'm really a very sweet guy."

He got up. Circling the couch, he went to the door, which Hippie opened. He paused there and said, "By the way, dear, we're going to give the wrist-slapping work to George Trent. He appreciates little gestures like that, does old George." He left the room. Hippie followed and closed them out.

Apple let the tension go out of his body. He sat on for a while before rising and stepping over to the couch. Sitting, he turned sideways and offered a tentative "Well."

Mona clasped her hands in her lap. Dully she echoed, "Well."

"Why don't you tell him?"

"I can't. It wouldn't be right."

"But he'll make you."

"No, he won't. At least, I hope he won't. I'm not a total mess."

They were both speaking softly. Apple edged closer. He said, "I don't think you're a mess at all. Everyone makes mistakes."

Mona glanced at him shyly. "I'm sorry," she murmured. "You know."

"Yes, I know."

"I'm glad I failed."

He smiled. "That's strange, so am I."

After briefly answering the smile, Mona said, "You don't seem like a gangster."

"Well, I don't feel like one. Don't think of myself as one. But yes, I suppose that's what it boils down to. Sort of."

"We all do things we don't like."

"That's true. With me, it's a way of making a living."

After a moment of quiet, in which there was no strain, Mona said, "My heart wasn't in it, that's the thing. I mean those failures. But I admit that sometimes it was pure stupidity. Such as that time in the car."

"Which time?"

"Up at the quarry. I ran on down ahead of you and moved the rocks away from the edge of the parking area. Rolled 'em over. Then I forgot, and climbed in the car with you."

There was fondness in the way Apple slowly shook his head. He said, "That wasn't very smart, I'm afraid."

"No. But mostly it was because, as I say, my heart wasn't truly in the project, even though I thought that you and George Trent were bad trouble for me."

"You guessed what we were after?"

"Oh no. That was a surprise. I thought you were KGB."

It all came out in a rush. She was like a child who had decided to give away every secret, having at long last found the right confidant. Eagerness, pride, and relief showed themselves as she talked. She whispered, glancing over one shoulder. She sat close and touched Apple frequently. She played with both plaits and with their ends painted various parts of her face. She had never looked younger, or more vulnerable.

There was little sequence in Mona's story. She jumped from a hoped-for future to a bitter present; in the middle of telling about espionage training, slipped back to a childhood event; blinked moistly over Mother Russia while slandering the dreariness of Moscow. It had all been kept in for a long time.

From the flow, Apple took and pieced together what was

pertinent. This he did unconsciously. He was intent on being a receptive, sympathetic audience. Often he said, "I understand."

Which was especially true when Mona admitted that the Ibiza job was her first mission. Before, she had been used only as a courier. They had sent her here, she knew, simply because there was no one else available who had the right languages to fit the cover, the necessary hotel experience, and a top loyalty rating.

"But I don't touch top in anything else."

"Neither . . ." Apple began. "I'm sorry. Go on."

She had loved the island, hated the job. Being here was like living in paradise, and she tried not to think of what hard drugs did to people. She had long ago made up her mind to stay in the sun, leave the work she loathed, while at the same time do nothing to harm her country or the secret service.

"But you're not allowed to quit," Mona said. "And once I got back behind the Iron Curtain I'd never get out again. I'd be doomed to Moscow and cold feet for the rest of my life."

Disappearance was the answer, she had concluded. She would vanish, and let her superiors make of it what they could—which would probably be to blame the espionage agents of some foreign power.

Playing the part of a Spaniard, she had regularly, secretly, taken the twenty-minute flight to the neighbouring island of Mallorca. There, in a resort town, she had rented a room and established another identity for herself. Meanwhile, again in secret, she had bought a small boat, which she had worked hard at learning to sail properly.

"I just about have it now. And I've added an outboard motor in case of problems. I keep the boat in a quiet cove at the other end of the island."

She had planned to leave right after the next monthly visit

by her Control. That would give her several weeks' leeway before the start of the hunt. The trail she hoped to render stone-cold by not leaving Ibiza by any of the regular channels, even in disguise.

"I was going to sail to Mallorca. I was going to get a job as a maid. I was going to live in the sun."

Apple pressed her hand.

She had been worried sick all along that the KGB would somehow get on to her plans, find out about the boat or her trips to the other island. She had felt at times that she was being watched, which feeling was strengthened when mysterious, snoopy George Trent showed up. She had got him to go to the quarry and attacked him from behind in the way she had been taught. When, some days later, she had returned only to find him gone, but with there having been no mention of bodies in the press, she had become convinced that the KGB were indeed involved and had dealt with the body themselves. She had hoped that somehow they would think foreign agents responsible.

"And it started all over again, Arnold, when I got your cable. But I didn't really want to kill anyone, even a deadly enemy. I just wanted to be free."

That part of the story had come near the beginning. Toward the end, she was telling of her parents, now dead, and her happy childhood. Finally she ran out of words.

As Mona gazed ahead, her smile faded. Quickly she looked behind at the door. "God," she said. "Time must be up. He'll be back soon."

"Yes," Apple said. "You have to give him what he wants."

She shook her head. "No."

"But why not?"

"Because it wouldn't be right. And anyway, for all I know, you people could still be the KGB, trying me out."

"It's a bit late to care, after everything you've told me."

"Somehow I trust you," Mona said. "But then, I'm not very good at this kind of thing."

"Listen, I swear to you that we're nothing to do with the KGB or Russia. Believe me."

"All right, I do," she said, shrugging defeatedly. "And yes, I suppose I'll tell him in the end. I don't think I could take torture. I'm not terribly brave. But I'll have to try to resist."

It was the word *torture* that did it. Apple made up his mind. Even though he thought Mona was being naïve to believe she could get away with her plan, sail across the sea and afterwards stay hidden from the vast Soviet network of eyes, he felt that she ought to be allowed to try. Besides, he was smitten. He wanted to take her in his arms and give her comfort.

Offering the same with tidings, Apple said, leaning forward and whispering, "I'll help you."

She turned to him. Their faces were close. In a low voice she asked, "Help me?"

"I'll get you away from here. I'll take you to your boat."

She stared. The seconds ticked by while Apple kept nodding an impatient yes yes yes. Mona said, "I believe you mean it."

"Of course I do," he said. It had all come so easily that he realized he had had it in mind for some time; that only a catalyst, a sign or word, had been needed.

There was a sound from beyond the door. A thud.

They both glanced behind. Still looking that way, Mona hissed, "Can you get away with it, Arnold?"

He whispered, "Yes, I think I know how." Of course he knew how.

"What if they kill you?"

"They won't," he said, getting up. "Are you ready?"

Smiling, she reached to take the hand he was holding out. "Yes."

A piece of grit squeaked underfoot on the tiles. Apple felt Mona's hand jerk, pull back, as if she wanted to freeze. He drew her on across the room in quiet and careful strides. The door stayed closed.

They reached the curtains. Recalling the way their brass rings had rattled when Fourteen had done the drawing, Apple took slow care about easing back one half of the drapes. The rings still complained. Mona whispered a terrified "Shhh."

Another thud came from beyond the door.

Apple looked through the glass. Seeing no one outside, he reached for the unlatched, battered french window.

Against the glass crashed a tall figure. Apple and Mona gasped. The window rumbled loudly.

The shaggy, sandy-coloured figure was Monico. Up on his hind legs, the dog stood man-height. He stared happily through the glass, eyes bright, tongue lolling, tail wafting back and forth.

Mona whimpered, "We're trapped."

"No, he's a friend of mine," Apple said. He pulled on the french-window half, which came easily with the push of Monico's weight. "He won't hurt you."

The dog dropped to all fours and backed off. Tail still wagging, he looked as though about to make another leap. Apple threw flapping gestures at him as he pushed Mona ahead through the gap, and once outside himself gave Monico a brief patting. He was immensely grateful for the dog's silent nature.

From a window farther along came the sound of coughing. Apple, not wanting to risk speech, nodded a direction at

Mona and went ahead to the steps, where she caught up. Monico appeared at his other side. They went down and across the grass.

There was a clang. It was followed by a cry. Since both had come from right beside Apple, shock almost caused him to cry out as well. But he only staggered off course. He recognized the cry as Mona's and the clang as happening when she had kicked the flashlight.

Still moving untidily forward, they both looked back. The room's interior was as before.

"Run!" Apple hissed.

They ran, all three, the humans with grim determination, the animal with gleeful bounds. Apple told himself, too late, that he ought to have picked up the flash. But that slice of moon was adequate to show the way through the trees.

Abruptly, Apple was taken by a feeling of exhilaration. The night, the shadows, the girl and dog, the risk factor, the fact of flight—these spelled romance and excitement. He had everything he wanted. He would have been happy to go on like this for hours.

But they came to the wall. Reminding himself that everything except the run was still alive, Apple said, "Up you get." He explained about the locked gates and his waiting car while stirruping Mona's foot with his hands and helping her climb.

Straddling the wall top, she began, "But why—"

What stopped her, and made Apple twitch, was a shout. It came from the house, which was seeable simply as a faint slice of light from one window. The muffled quality of the shout said that it had come from indoors. The escape had been discovered.

"Quick!" Mona said. "Give me your hand."

"I can manage. You go on."

"Okay." She went over the other side, making a clank as she stepped onto the car.

Apple found toeholds, climbed, swung one leg over the top. About to go on, swaying across, he swayed back on hearing the whine. He looked down.

At the foot of the wall sat Monico. He was staring up, shivering. His tail lay motionless on the grass. He whined again, a long and plaintive entreaty.

"Arnold," Mona called. "Please hurry."

Taking the dog along would be ridiculous, Apple thought. He swung his head as, from the house, came various noises: thuds, voices, running feet, a shouted order.

The dog whined.

Mona said, "Come on, come on."

Ridiculous, Apple thought, looking down. The dog rose and lifted itself, putting one front paw on the wall. The other leg dangled. The tail gave a slow wag in time with another whine.

More noises drew Apple's attention back toward the house. Car doors slammed over the sound of a starter. An engine roared. Brightness showed as headlights were switched on.

Her voice unsteady, Mona asked, "What's wrong, Arnold?"

Apple swung his leg over. I'm insane, he mused as he dropped to the ground. He scooped up the dog, heaved it to the top of the wall. Monico went from view and there was another clank from the Citroën.

The headlights were swinging around.

Apple began to climb. His foot slipped and he thunked down. Starting again with a different toehold, his height quickly got him within hand-grab of the top. Tree shadows swept past him as he went over on his belly. He used the car's wing as a step, calling, "All in. Get inside quick.

They're coming. But the gate should hold 'em up for another minute or so."

Mona got in the car. It was the wrong side; she slid across. Monico followed, bounding onto the front seat then over into the back. Apple slipped behind the wheel. He pressed the starter, switched on lights, slammed the jutting gear stick into reverse. He would have preferred going straight on, but the lane could turn out to be a dead end.

The motor started. Apple shot the car backwards. The main road clear, he arced onto it at speed. He braked to a snap-neck stop, clammered the stick into first, sent the 2CV into a great leap forward.

Mona was looking behind. She gasped, "They're here!"

Apple glanced in the rearview mirror. He met the affectionate gaze of Monico. After changing from screaming first into second, Apple swung the steering wheel sharply right, then back again. The dog was thrown out of the way.

Via the mirror Apple saw a pair of headlights. They were stationary, which puzzled him until he saw a figure running toward them; the car was waiting for whoever had unlocked the gates. When Apple next glanced back, seconds later, the lights were moving.

Mona asked, "Can you outrun them in this?"

Apple shook his head. "Not a chance."

"Oh," Mona said, following a pause. "Then we won't be able to get to the cove."

"Yes we will. I think I know a way. Hold tight."

They drove along sub-suburban streets, some of them without lighting, many of them unpaved, all of them made narrow by parked vehicles. There was no chance of the 2CV's being overtaken; and, by constantly taking corners, Apple was able to keep the chase car a minimum of one block behind.

Again, now, the Citroën seemed about to flop over on its side as a corner was attacked at speed. Mona lurched against Apple, heaved herself back into place, was slammed against the door when the car righted.

Apple had the steering wheel to hold on to. Monico was better off than either human. Wisely, at the first wild swerve, he had changed from seat to floor, where he lay with his back paws pressed into Apple's spine.

Monico had been the subject of the sole exchange to take place since leaving the villa behind. Mona had asked, "Whose dog is it anyway?" Apple had replied, "I haven't the faintest idea." He hadn't been surprised that Mona found this answer quite acceptable, and final.

They drove recklessly along a street that seemed to be a gathering place for lost potholes. The 2CV bounced gaily. Mona crouched low, Apple held himself down by pressing one hand against the roof.

The road levelled out. Mona, who had continually divided her attention between behind and ahead, said, her voice breathless, "That slowed 'em a bit."

"Their car's too good for rough stuff."

"They wouldn't try shooting at us, would they?"

"Wouldn't dare," Apple said. "Not here in public areas." He didn't know if that was true or not.

"But how're you going to get away with all this, Arnold?"

"Explain in a minute." Driving this way, with frequent switches of direction, he preferred not to talk. He was, however, thinking, though his thoughts were removed from the here and now. Thinking also helped to keep his mind off the consequences of what he was doing. Apple was beginning to feel slightly unnerved.

He reminded himself that he had always wanted a dog, so that was all right from his own point of view. From the other,

Monico seemed to feel that he had found a friend, so that was all right too. Ownership would have to be checked into, plus the quarantine situation in the UK, but—

Mona shrieked, "Look out!"

At the crossroads they were bearing down on swiftly, a tourist coach was nosing into view from the right. The interior was packed. The windows couldn't keep in the bedlam of a German beer-hall song.

Aware that he was being more of a show-off than a wise driver, Apple zoomed toward the coach's nose. He cut in front. There was a clang as his back bumper hit, the car skewed around, the coach began screeching to a halt.

Grinning to show that his heart wasn't hammering, Apple scraped through a fast gear change and shot away. Mona took her hand from her mouth and gagged, "Christ."

The mirror showed Apple that the coach had stopped; it was blockingly across the junction. The noise from the interior was not a song.

"We've gained at least a minute," Apple said with acted brightness. He was more unnerved than ever.

Nor did it improve his feelings when, three quick-taken blocks further on, he came to the main road he had been seeking. He told himself he would have had to reach it sooner or later.

He made the turn and pressed his foot to the floor. The road flat, straight, and wide, he said, "Listen. Don't worry about me. Everything's going to work out fine." He nodded. He was in need of assurance, if only from himself.

"What will you say?" Mona asked, looking behind.

"That you got a judo hold on me. A special one. They'll buy that. You've had KGB training and know all those clever holds, whereas the boss knows they're all a mystery to me. See?"

"It's good so far, yes."

Yes, Apple told himself, it was good. In fact, it could be used as that best form of defence—attack. He would say the grip was one that was new to him. It hadn't been invented when he had done his training, years ago. Angry, he would say, "This is what comes of not keeping your people right up to the minute, of not giving them regular refresher courses. So don't blame me. It's not my fault." He would lay it on thick.

Mona said, "But I couldn't have kept any kind of hold on you if we were running."

Apple shook his head. "No no. You used it only long enough to take my revolver away from me. You made me obey you at gunpoint."

"That's fine—so long as you have a gun."

He brought the revolver from under his shirt. "There you are."

"Thank you," Mona said. She slipped it into her cleavage. "I don't like guns."

"Neither do I."

"Yes, Arnold, I think you'll get away with it. But how can I even begin to thank you?" She straightened. "It's coming. The car."

"Sooner than I thought," Apple muttered. His eyes were nervously scanning the road far ahead, straining to find a particular landmark.

"And this isn't a public area." She meant that there were no places of habitation siding the straight highway; nothing to inhibit gunfire.

The Citroën was trembling with effort. It could go no faster, despite its accelerator being flat to the mat. Apple sat leaned forward over the wheel. To encourage speed he rocked back and forth, like someone giving body nods. His confidence was ebbing.

Ahead, coloured lights gleamed. Apple needed to see them

so badly that he thought they were beautiful. Even so, he didn't know if he could get that far before being overtaken.

Mona said tensely, "They're catching up."

"I can see that."

"We'll never do it. There's miles and miles to go yet."

Apple riffled through a mental file, going over the methods for dealing with a chase car. They all involved lethal tactics or sophisticated equipment. But the lights ahead were closer now; the lights belonging to the service station.

He said, "Hold on. We're nearly there."

"Where?"

"We're turning off this road."

"They're almost here."

The rearview mirror showed a clear picture of the chase car, its headlights on dim. Apple could make out the faces of Angus Watkin, Maria, and the two agents. He was glad to see that the driver was Hippie, who might not be as familiar with the way as Fourteen.

The service station was close. Three cars were standing on its forecourt, by the pumps.

Apple waited until the last possible second. With the other car mere yards behind, he slammed on his brakes. They screamed. There came an answer-seeming scream from behind. Apple released the brake pedal and viciously swung the wheel.

The Citroën roared onto the forecourt. Noting with part of his attention that the other car was going straight on as it slowed, Apple swung the steering wheel in the opposite direction. He made full lock, his hands pounding down like a chopping masseur's.

The car shot past the waiting vehicles. Apple saw a blur of lights, heard an attendant shout—and then he was off the forecourt and on a dark, decrepit road.

With a fast glance back toward the highway, he was in time to glimpse the chase car; it was reversing in order to follow into the service station.

Apple stayed in second gear until its shrilling became unbearable and the speed constant. He hit third, where he intended staying, for maximum power on a short run.

Mona turned and kneeled on the seat. She said, "Not yet."

"The pump jockey might get in the way. Every second counts."

"You're great, Arnold. You really are."

"Yes," he said absently, head forward, peering. He saw the slanting turnoff. As he was steering into it, Mona said, "They've come out."

The 2CV's headlights picked out the gate. Apple wondered if it might be locked. It didn't matter, he decided. Even the briefest delay would be fatal.

Again, Apple waited until the last moment before stamping hard on the brake pedal, and again there was a screamed complaint. The Citroën came to a shuddering halt with its front bumper a foot from the gate.

"Out!" Apple shouted as he switched off the lights. The motor he left running; it was the wrong thing to do, therefore useful as a confuser. Always do the unexpected, Training Four taught.

Apple, Mona, and Monico, they leapt out. In various fashions from clearing jump to scramble, they got over the gate. As they set off at a run across the meadow, Apple said, "I ought to have asked you before."

"What?"

"Can you fly a helicopter?"

"Of course. Part of basic training."

"Thought so. Spies can do everything."

Mona panted, "We're going in a chopper?"

"You are." If, he thought, it's still there. "Your hostage is no good to you from here on."

"I get you."

Listen, he would say, she told *me* which way to go. She must have followed us, that time I was brought out here by Fourteen. I don't like to complain about security arrangements, but . . .

They pounded on over the field, with Monico bounding friskily. They ran in a tunnel of shadow as the chase car's headlights appeared and came closer: the 2CV acted as a block. All that the lights hit was the cluster of prefabricated buildings.

The car stopped. Figures were getting out, Apple saw when he glanced back. He grabbed Mona's wrist and dragged her forward, but eased off slightly on realizing that she could fall, that she didn't have his long-legged speed.

They reached the first building. It spread out on either side into the headlights' brightness. Reluctantly Apple towed Mona into the light. They went around the corner, then to the rear. The helicopter was there.

Apple ran ahead. He yanked open the door. "Get in, get in."

Mona climbed up onto the seat. As she bent over the controls, the revolver made it appear that she had three breasts. Apple wished he didn't think about things like that. He was about to tell her where to find the right switch, pointing, when with a whine the blades began to turn.

The motor started. Everything began to dance in the wind from above. Smiling, Mona turned to Apple. They were level. Reaching out, Apple took her by the plaits and drew her to meet his lean. He kissed her hard on the mouth.

Mona's lips were eloquent. Apple wished he had the leisure to take it all in. But time was snap-finger short. He released his hold and eased back. Crouching because of the blades, he continued to reverse. He put his hands on top of his head: a man under the threat of a gun.

Mona broke off the solemn eye contact. She pulled the door in. The helicopter jerked, jerked again, rose a yard in the air, paused there, and then swept upward.

Apple's clothes were beginning to settle from the wind's panic as he was abruptly caught between two sets of headlights. The 2CV had been brought as well. He lowered his arms, though continuing to gaze after the rising aircraft.

All Apple's nervousness had gone, along with his pang of regret at the goodbye. His confidence was back in force. He felt, in fact, fabulous. He had a magnified version of the exhilaration he had been taken by earlier, when running through the trees at the villa.

It's all happening, he thought. The lights, the urgent cars, a helicopter, a glamorous foreign spy, the mission successfully completed, the romance and excitement. It's all happening, and it's happening here, now, to me—me, Appleton Porter, secret agent.

Car doors slammed. Apple turned. As he did, he put on a frown of anger. Inside, he was singing.

EPILOGUE

Dear Sam,

I imagine you would be interested in knowing the result of that little problem in Ibiza. Most of it is outlined in the enclosed report, which, of course, has had all danger details removed, even though it comes to you by courier, and even though you will B & F it along with this note immediately after reading.

I do not, by the by, recall the night in Lisbon which you mentioned in your letter to me of a week ago. I think you must be confusing me with someone else.

However. Ibiza.

As it turned out, I took a personal look into the affair, for I happened to be in that general area in connection with the NATO nonsense, and I needed a break from hobnobbing with Our Gallant Allies.

There is, as you know, always the problem of getting rid of any detainees once a mission has run its course. In the old days it was different. But things have changed, I'm happy to say. I hate violence.

We had no further use for our detainee once we had it out of her that she was running the operation, that we need search no higher. Also, we had managed to plant in her head a snippet of misinformation, which will now be causing concern in the Kremlin. The how-why-what of said false information I cannot, I'm afraid, pass on to you.

What I can tell you, Sam, is that the grapevine brings us word of a Moscow claim that someone (they hint at the CIA) has lifted one of their agents. At the same time, they don't seem particularly interested in getting the lady back.

I'm most intrigued with this lie of Moscow's and am busy playing with ideas.

But to the admirable Porter. He was, as I had hoped, the right man for the job. He served his dual purpose well. The first you will read about in the enclosed document. The second was to get the lady off our hands and safely into those of her Control. To that end, for our part, we let Porter know where he could conveniently find a helicopter, though in the event he did not, as expected, use it himself, but let the lady take over from there. We also played the ruthless line, and threatened torture.

For Porter's part—well, it was taken care of by his personality.

The first half of the mission was a total success. I am confident that the second half will be equally satisfying.

It was for said second part that Porter had to be used as the dummy. The KGB have a new truth drug, which we are desperate to get hold of. They will be sure to use it on Porter, in a way that will leave him unaware of what has happened. They will want to know, naturally, if their agent's escape was genuine or faked. He will only be able to say that it was genuine. And this will give us the opportunity to try and get hold of the drug—after they have dealt with Porter—by using one of the usual methods that won't, one hopes, be suspicious: car accident, female enticement, etc. You know the kind of thing.

We are left with two trifling problems. The first, business, concerns that helicopter. The Royal Air Force people in Gibraltar are nagging us to return the damn thing, while the

Spanish authorities are asking a lot of awkward questions. The latter will fade in the fullness of time. The former is an accommodation which we cannot manage, there being considerable damage to the aircraft. It seems that at the cove, where a launch or a submarine would no doubt have been waiting to take her off, the lady brought the helicopter down in a tree.

The second problem is personal—and the reason that I am writing this note rather than buttonholing you in the club within the next day or two.

The operation supervisor rented a dog, suitably useless so as not to discourage Porter. It obviously took a liking to the supervisor, for (the gate had been left open) it followed his car to the takeoff point. I was just starting on a show tirade against Porter when the stupid animal attacked me. The stitches come out in a few days. Meanwhile, I have to stay off that leg.

Oddly, the men who are watching Porter clock-round, waiting for the expected KGB approach, report that he has arranged to have a dog flown here from Ibiza and be put into kennels for the obligatory quarantine period. One can only assume that it's the same animal, and that some sort of revenge is planned against it for the attack on my person.

Although I've said it before, I'll say it again: he's a curious fellow, this Appleton Porter.

        As always,

            Angus

Marc Lovell is the author of three previous Appleton Porter novels, *Spy on the Run, The Spy with His Head in the Clouds,* and *The Spy Game,* as well as many others, including *Hand over Mind* and *A Voice from the Living.* Mr. Lovell has lived on the island of Majorca for the last twenty years.